©
Copyri

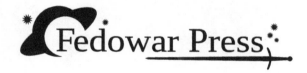

www.FedowarPress.com
Fedowar Press, LLC

ISBN-13 (Digital): 978-1-7366865-4-6
ISBN-13 (Paperback): 978-1-7366865-5-3

Edited by Renée Gendron
Cover Design by JL Peridot
Interior Design by D.W. Hitz

STAR CROSSED

AN ANTHOLOGY OF ROMANTIC SCIENCE FICTION

FEATURING STORIES BY

B.K. BASS   IAN MARTÍNEZ CASSMEYER
RENÉE GENDRON   D.W. HITZ
PAMELA JAMES   NIKKI MITCHELL
J.L. PERIDOT   L.A. STINNETT

Contents

FOREWORD

I had the privilege and pleasure of working with writers from Twitter's writing community for the romantic science fiction anthology Star Crossed.

Participants of the anthology were given a picture of two astronauts in space suits standing on spires over-looking a moon planet. Clouds encompass the majority of the spires. The astronauts face the dark side of the planet, and there are illuminated cities. To the side of the planet is a sun.

Authors were instructed to write a story based on a picture that had at least one romantic element. A romantic element can include a loving glance at their partners or romance being a driver of the plot.

To respect the author's voice, some stories in this anthology use American spelling and others use British spelling. This means some words may appear to be misspelt when they are spelt differently. I'm grateful for your understanding in this respect.

All proceeds of this anthology are donated to the

International Red Cross.

On behalf of the authors, I sincerely hope you enjoy these stories.

Kind regards,
Renée Gendron

Far From Home
by B.K. Bass

I press my hand against the sterile white wall, fathoming that just a finger's width of human ingenuity separates me from the unforgiving vacuum of space. As the capsule rotates, I peer through the tiny viewport towards Wayland. A faint halo of sunlight crowns the planet as shadow engulfs the near side. A constellation of pinpoints light the surface as the cities back home press away the darkness of night.

Legends tell of people coming to Wayland from the stars long ago. Nobody knows if there is truth behind these myths, shrouded in time as they are, but the hopeful among us yearn for a day we may learn where we came from. The lonely among us simply hope we aren't alone in the cold expanse of space.

I settle back into my seat and check my instruments,

bolstered by the knowledge that I am the first to break the chains of gravity which hold us to Wayland and set out to explore the unknown. Would it be that I was to venture among those very stars mirrored by the twinkling lights of home, but not yet. Instead, I'm to undertake the nascent steps of exploring the one celestial body currently within our reach: our moon, Eros. For thousands of years, humanity has looked up to this glittering, violet orb in the night sky. It is as mysterious as its namesake; a mythological figure from some long-forgotten culture in our muddled pre-history. And now I am to be the first man to visit it.

"This is Captain Razgall to Control. I'm making my deceleration burn now."

The radio crackles back with a voice broken by static, "Affirm that, Razgall. Stars bless your landing."

Wayland shrinks in the viewport as I flip the switch to ignite the capsule's main engine. I am pressed firmly into my seat as the entire craft shakes and vibrates around me. The burn only lasts a few moments, just long enough to slow the capsule so it might be caught by Eros' thick atmosphere.

I check one of the grainy, black and white monitors on the console and catch my first glimpse of the moon from an external camera. Undulating clouds flow over the entire surface, broken only by the periodical peak of a jagged mountain worn slender by the tempestuous, eternal storms.

Anticipation wells in my chest, a tightening that

momentarily takes my breath away, as I am about to be the first man to see the surface of Eros. We'd sent probes, but thus far their telemetry has been unable to pierce the thick clouds that shroud the moon. What lay beneath that roiling sea of vapors, none knows for sure, but the mountain peaks give us hints. Too narrow to land a probe on, we'd been unable to collect samples. However, visual inspections show they are likely made of similar minerals to those at home. A reassuring thought for one readying to set foot on an unknown surface.

A new rumbling shakes the capsule as the clouds and peaks grow nearer in the monitor. As I enter the upper atmosphere of Eros, I check my straps, cinch them tight, and ready myself for the descent. My hands hover over the control sticks on either side of my seat, with which I will guide the craft to land. Assuming, that is, there is land to guide it to.

I know—we all know—there is a probability my mission will end in earnest before it even begins. Knowing little to nothing of the moon's surface, there may be no safe harbor for my small craft. I may find myself dashed upon a jagged mountainside among unforgiving peaks and valleys. I may find those jagged mountains jutting from an endless sea like the legs of an upturned crab in the shallows. That's why I was chosen, among all the hopefuls, for this mission. Having no spouse, no children, and very little living family; I have few to mourn my passing.

I reach out against a fresh pull of gravity from the moon, fighting against the shaking ship, and grab hold of a single photograph tucked into the console. A man who looks much like myself stands before a simple clay-brick home. He smiles broadly as he holds aloft a small child. Beside him stands a modestly-dressed woman, and before them two adolescents mug for the camera. My brother and his family — the only real family I have.

The radio crackles to life again, but the words are lost in static. Outside the viewport, swirls of violet, white, and blue vapors whip by the thin glass. I am entering the moon's cloud layer, and whatever message Control tried to send is lost beyond the impenetrable barrier I now plunge blindly through.

A dull thud reverberates through the capsule and it jerks suddenly as the drag chute is released to slow my descent. I check a monitor displaying the view from several lower-facing cameras. The four images split the screen. But for the borders between each, I wouldn't be able to tell where one begins and the other ends. Swirling clouds are all they show.

The altimeter flutters near zero and an alarm warns me I'm about to crash into the surface, but the laser and coupled infrared sensor simply can't penetrate the thick clouds. Data rolls across a nearby screen as external sensors scoop up bits of cloud and measure the air around the craft. Nearby, red text flashes on another screen with two expected, yet terrifying words: "Telemetry failure". I am, for the first time ever, truly alone.

4

I push that horrid thought from my mind and focus on the instruments and the monitors, waiting for my first glimpse of what lies below Eros's clouds, if anything at all does. Thoughts of endlessly hurtling through the violet eddies flutter through my mind, even though all rational thought argues against such a notion. Still, the mind fills in the gaps, and there's a lot about the moon we simply don't know.

Then, just as suddenly as the clouds engulfed the capsule, I am free of them. All four cameras show clear images for the first time. I glance out the viewport for a moment. Bright, violet clouds swirled with blue, more vibrant from below than they were from above, rise away from me. Or rather, I fall away from them.

Reminded of the urgency of the moment, I tear my gaze away from the breathtaking view and focus on the monitors. The altimeter holds a steady number near thirty-thousand feet, but this number is quickly shrinking. Now free of the clouds, my velocity is increasing.

I flip open a switch's protective cover and toggle it. A series of dull thuds run through the capsule as secondary drag chutes are released, and I clench my teeth as the craft jerks and slows. I still have little time to act, and much to do. The cameras show what we had both feared and expected most; a jagged landscape ravaged by constant storms. Below me there are no windswept plains or expanse of desert, flat tundra or gentle hills. The peaks which puncture the clouds around the moon are merely the tips of colossal mountains, and between them lay only narrow valleys. Rivers run through these, a web of waterways that criss-cross the surface as far as the cameras can see.

And there I find hope. Between the mountains, alongside the rivers, there are pockets of flat land. Perhaps the rivers once rose higher and cut these narrow swaths. But in these valleys, another problem presents itself. Surrounding the rivers and hugging the feet of the mountains lay what appears to be thick forests.

I roll my eyes and let out a cynical huff as I pick up my helmet from its resting place, lower it over my head, and secure it to my spacesuit. "Nothing's ever easy," I mutter within the confines of the glass and metal bubble.

I grasp the control sticks and nudge one of them gently. A short hiss, muffled by the capsule and my helmet, reassures me the thrusters are working. I press the stick firmer and longer, and a long hiss is accompanied by a gentle swaying. The images on the monitor pan as I guide the craft toward one of the valleys. I'm still too high to see if there's a large enough break in the trees to land, so one valley seems as good as any other. With short bursts of the thrusters, I guide my lonely craft towards one of them.

The near-vertical cliffs of the mountains frame my view, an imposing reminder of just how little of the surface isn't dominated by them. Below, the valley grows larger. The river wends and weaves through the terrain. With no lowlands to run to—and from what I've seen, no sea to fill—the river must simply run between the mountains until it meets one of its compatriots. Where the water goes, I haven't the foggiest. I add that to the thousands of questions I'll hope to answer once I'm on the ground.

I grin at my still-hopeful thinking, despite the nearly-impossible situation looming larger in the monitors. The forest surrounding the river grows larger and fills the screen. I switch off three of the cameras and a single image stretches to fill the frame. I toggle another switch, and a final set of parachutes deploy. This last trio of red fabric domes are now all that keep me from being dashed on the surface below.

Two-thousand feet. Before long, the capsule will be settling onto the surface. Whether it comes to a gentle rest on landing struts or crashes through the trees is yet to be seen. I steer the craft towards the flattest portion of land, though even this slopes towards the river. Should the capsule not secure a foothold on landing, it will surely tumble into the waters.

One-thousand feet. I nudge the craft towards a thinner patch of trees. There's hope for a clearing there. One thumb hovers over the ignition for the main engine.

Five-hundred feet. There, amid an endless sea of green now filling the monitor, is a gap in the canopy. I steer towards it, even though fitting the capsule between the trees at this speed is tantamount to threading a needle in a windstorm. Still, it's my only chance.

Two-hundred feet. I thumb the toggle for the main engine. Orange flames obscure the camera below as the capsule rumbles and shakes. The craft slows for the final leg of its descent. I sit back, grasp my harness, and squeeze my eyes shut. There's nothing to do now but pray to the stars.

An alarm klaxon sounds from the altimeter, warning me of imminent contact with the surface. The volume of the screeching alarm competes against the thrumming of my own pulse in my ears.

I open my eyes. Twenty-five feet. I turn off the main engine, and as soon as I do there's a sudden jerk as the landing struts meet the ground. After the cacophony of swirling instruments, warning alarms, roaring wind, and rumbling engines; there is nothing but silence.

There's a dull hiss as the capsule door unseals and the sterile, controlled atmosphere inside the craft is inundated by the higher-pressure of the air outside. I press open the hatch and swing it aside as pneumatics lower a ladder towards the ground. From the opening, all I can see is an ocean of strange trees. Angular, almost geometrically aligned branches sway as harsh winds bellow through the valley. Narrow, needle-like leaves crowd the branches, tangled into a mass of impenetrable greenery shuddering in the wind — resembling a mosaic running through a blender. Below, an uneven rocky surface is covered in verdant, moss-like vegetation.

Turning, I place one foot on a rung already slippery from the moisture in the air. I carefully climb down until I stand on the lowest bar. Taking a deep breath before leaving my only tie to home behind, I set foot on the alien surface. Loose gravel and dirt crunches under my booted foot. The spongy vegetation squishes and water runs across the rocks. Moisture is beading across my suit, most notably obscuring the visor of my helmet.

As I turn away from the ladder, I wipe the cloying condensation from my face shield, then check the atmospheric readouts on a panel set into my suit's forearm. All the familiar elements are there; mostly nitrogen and oxygen, with some carbon dioxide and methane. Notably, there are more than trace levels of hydrogen and helium, though still less than one percent of the makeup. Those, combined with a water vapor content that tops out the scale, explain the purple clouds.

Beading moisture again obstructs my view. But through the film, I see the one thing we had all held hope for against all reason. A bright, blinking green light flashes on the readout, indicating a breathable atmosphere.

I wipe away the beading liquid again and manually check the readouts one more time. Everything checks out. The minor gasses vary a bit, but not so much as to cause any concern. The air is thick with humidity, and to call the temperature brisk would be understating things. But, there is nothing to indicate a dangerous environment.

I should keep my helmet on. I should do more tests and access my situation. But, I can't see a damned thing with the moisture beading on my visor.

I reach to my neck and blindly unfasten the helmet. I hold my breath and close my eyes by instinct rather than conscious thought as I raise the dome away from my head. Cold air rushes in and caresses my face. I take a deep breath and almost choke. Words can hardly describe the thickness of it. Even the most humid day near the sea on Wayland is nothing compared to this. I open my eyes and immediately have to blink away tears as they water in response. It feels almost as if I'm swimming, even though I know otherwise.

I take another, shallower breath. My lungs protest, but hold the air down. I want to gag on the thickness of it, but I fight the urge. After a few more breaths, the air comes easier. I keep reminding myself the readouts say it's safe as I fight the panic breathing the strange air fills me with.

And then the scent hits me. Or scents, I should say. Filling the air is the familiar smell that precedes a storm, but mixed with that is a spicy, pungent odor. Likely from the trees, or the moss below my feet? I'll have to investigate further. Another thing on the list of questions about this place.

And just as that list of a thousand questions starts rolling through my mind, something crashes through the vegetation nearby. Something large. I turn towards the edge of the clearing, my hand hovering over the sidearm on my hip, when the most unexpected sight greets me. Emerging from the thick undergrowth, a woman runs into the clearing. She's clad from head to toe in some sort of animal hides, the black material clashing with her alabaster skin, yet matching her dark hair. She's looking over her shoulder as she sprints through the clearing, and she crashes into me.

I catch her and hold her up as she almost falls over my feet. She looks up at me from below my shoulder and her green eyes meet mine — wide and filled with what could be nothing other than sheer terror. Before my heart has a chance to skip a beat, she speaks a single word in plain Waylish: "Run!"

Before I can blink, she tears from my grasp and dashes through the clearing and into the trees. I begin to follow when another crashing noise spins me around.

Another form emerges from the trees, massive and hulking. Thick legs spur it forth aided by long, equally girthy arms. Blue scales cover its head, knees, hands, and forearms. Everywhere else bristles with coarse, silver fur. It stops in the clearing and towers over me as it seems to puzzle out the strange contraption arrayed before it — my capsule.

Its fang-filled maw gapes wide as it lets out a terrible screech. Then, as if offended by the intrusion, it lifts both trunk-like arms and bats the capsule aside.

My heart nearly explodes in my chest as my only hope of returning home rolls end-over-end down the river valley, now little more than a broken and battered shell.

My gaze turns and meets the beast's. My hand hovers again near my sidearm, trembling as I stare into the alien monster's tiny, glistening red eyes.

Then its maw gapes anew to release another blood-chilling cry, and the single word spoken by the mysterious woman floods my mind: Run!

I pivot and dash into the trees. Thunder follows me as the massive creature plods across the clearing and crashes through the foliage on my heels. My feet beat out a frenetic pace. My breath puffs before me in the cold air. Soon, all I can hear is my own pulse thrumming in my ears.

I duck under strange, angular branches. I dash around moss-covered stones. A narrow stream cuts across my path, and I leap it, only to slide on the moist gravel on the opposite bank. My feet slide from under me and I fall to my knees. Even through the thick, insulated space suit, I feel the rocks of Eros dig into the flesh of my legs. My hands catch me and those rocks dig through the gloves into my palms.

I dare a glance over my shoulder and see the shadow of the beast emerging from the forest. Light muted by the eternal cloud cover glistens on the vapors cloying upon its fur. Gravel and dirt scatters as massive fists beat into the ground, both guiding and propelling the monster with preternatural speed.

A hand grasps my arm and I tear my gaze away from the monster. The black-clad woman with alabaster skin stands over me, her eyes wide and fearful. She's pleading wordlessly for me to rise. For me to run. She tugs at my arm as she backs away, the thick leather of her hide boots digging trenches in the bank of the stream as she struggles to drag me to my feet.

She need not implore me long. I find my feet once again below me, and we run through the razor-sharp needles of the forest together. Blood trickles across my face as I dash through the growth without care. I barely feel the million tiny cuts, as the cold air has numbed my flesh.

Despite the cold air on my face, my suit warms me. And as I run, that warmth becomes heat. The insulation struggles to wick away the sweat that's bathing my body.

My heart races. Fear drives the drumbeat. That, and driving my legs past exhaustion to take just one more step through the underbrush. But as the crashing signs of the beast's pursuit begin to fade behind me, something else spurs my pulse onward.

Ahead, the mysterious woman leaps and ducks and strides through the strange forest as if a beast herself, born to this very task. Her slender, powerful legs peak out from the draped furs with every step she takes. Her fair skin is unblemished as she expertly weaves between the branches of clawing foliage. Her dark hair glistens violet in the strange glow of the alien day.

Suddenly, she slows and turns toward the mountain. I follow, craning my neck to see the monolithic structure rising into the clouds above us. The ground rises as our place slows, and our mad dash becomes a careful climb. We're both using hands as well as feet now in what feels to be a mimicry of the beast's gait. I steady myself against slippery, moss-covered stones with my hands as my feet dig into the gravely rise.

She turns and meets my eyes, then waves me onward. She can't mean to climb the peak, can she? I have no choice but to trust. To follow. My breath comes in ragged gasps as I struggle to breathe in the thick air. Even if I were inclined to question her destination, I think I'd hardly find the air to speak.

And as our climb seems to be at an end with the cliff-side rising almost vertically above us, she sidles around it into a crack in the stone. I follow into the shadows, and soon find myself stepping out of the dull sunlight and into utter darkness. I fumble blindly to retrieve a flashlight from a pocket in my suit, but before I can pull it out sparks fly before me, accompanied by the crack of two stones striking one another.

Another crack rings through the small space and echoes ahead of me, and another spark lights the darkness for a moment. Then, a smoldering, and a flame. The woman holds a short branch aloft as it sizzles and burns. The fire sputters for a moment in the thick, moist air, then roars to life as some sort of pitch bubbles on its head.

I've almost run into her in the darkness, and she places a firm hand on my chest to stop me even as I struggle to maintain my balance. Behind her, a tunnel stretches out into the void. Around us, smooth stone walls shelter us. Carvings line the walls, depicting scenes of figures hunting with spears and bows. Others show people grouped together in what could only be underground villages. Some show hulking monsters giving chase, and smaller forms hiding beneath the ground from them.

I look back. The tunnel is too narrow for the beast to follow, or so I hope. Even so, I no longer hear it crashing through the trees. Maybe it's given up the chase?

I turn back to my mysterious stranger. Her hand remains on my chest. I gently grasp her arm with my own hand, though I know not if I do this to reassure her or myself. We stand closer than the narrow tunnel dictates, and our eyes meet one another's. She runs her hands across my space suit, seemingly mystified by the synthetic fabrics and metal fittings. I hold my arms out and allow her to explore. She laughs, and again our gazes meet. As I look down at her wide, emerald eyes, the realization that I am not alone washes over me. Even more poignant than that, a realization for all the people of Wayland occurs to me: we are not alone.

About B.K. Bass

B.K. Bass is the author of over a dozen works of science fiction, fantasy, and horror inspired by the pulp fiction magazines of the early 20th century and classic speculative fiction. He is a student of history with a particular focus on the ancient, classical, and medieval eras. B.K. has a lifetime of experience with a specialization in business management and human relations, and served in the U.S. Army as a Nuclear, Chemical, and Biological Operations Specialist. When B.K. isn't dreaming up new worlds to explore, he spends his time as a bookworm, film buff, strategy gamer, and caretaker to an unusual number of cats and one small dog who thinks she's a cat.

Find out more about B.K. Bass below.

Website: bkbass.com

Twitter: @B_K_Bass.

Honor, Duty, Love
by L.A. Stinnett

Aubry sat on the deck outside the geodesic dome cabin. She removed her oxygen mask to sip her cup of tea and looked out over the lake through the fading twilight. The air on Kashim was much thinner than on Earth, and she became light-headed without the mask. Strange orange and black fish with long wing-like fins thrust themselves into the air, catching insects buzzing over the water. The smell of roasting wild qualma bird filled the air, making her stomach turn sour. On Earth, they stopped slaughtering animals for food long ago. She couldn't stand the sight of the carcass browning on a spit over the fire pit.

"You doing okay, kacha?" her fiancè Jaxon said, using a Kashimi term of endearment. The firelight showed off his dusky grey skin. Pearlescent blue eyes gazed at her beneath prominent brow ridges.

"Yes, just a little stomach upset. Do we really have to eat the poor bird? There's a food processor in the cabin."

He approached and kneeled before her, laying his hand on her stomach. "Kashimi babies need lots of animal protein to develop properly. Your food processor is all plant-based."

"He's only half Kashimi," Aubry said, smiling at him. He'd been so happy when the scan revealed they were having a son.

"Well, the Kashimi half needs all the protein he can get," he said, pulling the mask away and leaning forward to kiss her. His lips were rough against hers, but she'd learned to love their coarse feeling against her skin.

Jaxon returned to the firepit and removed the bird from the spit, laying it on a stone slab to carve the meat from the bone. He scooped a pile of thick pink slices onto a plate, along with some roasted vegetables, and laid the meal before her.

Aubry dug her fork in tentatively, still hesitant about eating meat. Jaxon gave her an encouraging look. She exhaled and took a small bite, finding it had a sweet, almost honey-flavored taste.

"What do you think of my outdoor cooking?" he said, raising a forkful of food to his mouth.

"It has a very pleasant flavor, would go great with a nice Pinot Noir," she said wistfully.

"You know any alcohol would kill the baby. Kashimi fetuses at this early stage can't tolerate it," he said sternly.

"I know. Just looking forward to being able to have a little wine once the baby's born."

"Have you decided on a name?" Jaxon said.

"Well, I was thinking about naming him after my great-grandfather, but don't you want a say in naming our son?"

"I told you before, the women in our culture choose the names for our children. What was your great-grandfather's name?"

"Logan," Aubry said, smiling as she took another bite of food. He'd been a big influence on her as a child. He gave her her first diary, instilling the importance of journaling daily life and thoughts.

"That's a grand name. I'm proud our son will carry on your great-grandfather's honor."

A pang of guilt filled her heart. "I'm sorry he can't bear your family name."

Jaxon laid his plate down. Sitting up straight, he squared his shoulders. "I told you before my royal title means nothing to me. I'm thirty-sixth in line of succession. I will never rule Kashim. I was just going to be married off for some political alliance. I want to wed for love, not duty."

"But you gave up so much — life in the palace. Your royal position . . ."

Jaxon approached and kneeled before her. "I gladly

gave it up." He took a moment to look around at the surroundings. "One of my uncles regularly brought me to this cabin with his wife and my cousins when I was a boy. It became my favorite place in all of Kashim. I preferred it here over palace life. My uncle was like me, long down in the line of succession. He liked his independence and instilled that in me too. I'd rather have a life with you than be a royal figurehead at tedious diplomatic engagements."

"But you won't even have the cabin anymore. They're banishing you from Kashim," Aubry said, blinking back tears.

Jaxon took her hand, bringing it to his lips for a kiss. The roughness of his lips against her knuckles sent tingles up her arm.

"Part of the reason I joined the Galactic Alliance fighter squadrons was to get away from here, see the galaxy and visit new worlds."

"You sound like an Alliance recruitment video," she said.

"Just doing my duty as a member of the GA," he said, grinning. "Know that wherever we end up, as long as we're together, I'll be the happiest man in the universe." He reached out to wipe a tear from her cheek.

Aubry smiled and looked into his eyes. "I love you, and you've made my life the happiest it's ever been, but I'm not sure I'm worth costing you so much." She dropped her gaze, remorse settling heavily in her bosom.

Jaxon gently placed his hands on her shoulders and laid her back on the outdoor lounge. "Let me show you how much you mean to me." He slowly undid the buttons on her blouse, fingertips lightly brushing her skin, causing her to shiver. Leaning forward, he pressed his lips against her chest, breath warm against her flesh. Aubry sighed deeply in anticipation of his tender attentions.

Morning sickness forced her out of bed early the following day. She was only a month and a half along in her pregnancy and was looking forward to the end of the daily nausea and vomiting. In the bathroom, Aubry rinsed out her mouth at the sink and brushed her teeth. She grabbed a hairband and wound her auburn strands into a bun.

Her backpack sat near the door. She unzipped it and went through the contents, double-checking to make sure she had everything needed for their hike to Adoration Spires. She set aside her well-worn leather diary and removed her small mask to slip a full-face version over her head. Aubry twisted the nozzle on the O2 tank allowing the higher oxy mixture to flow. She inhaled deeply, feeling relief at getting the full oxygen load she needed. The spires were at a much higher elevation than the cabin; she'd never make it without the full face mask.

Aubry carefully packed everything away again and approached the food processor, punching in the command for lemongrass tea. She sat at the table and looked out over the fog-shrouded lake. A large dromu, a heavy-bodied deer-like animal with twisting spikes protruding from its head, waded into the water to graze on plants floating at the surface. Aubry rose to retrieve her steaming mug when the processor dinged. She wrapped a robe around herself and stepped onto the deck. Everything was so quiet; the only sound was the water gently lapping the sandy shore. This trip was their last before leaving Kashim for good. Jaxon wanted to show her Adoration Spires before they left. He said it was the most beautiful spot in the entire galaxy.

She was going to miss this cozy cabin by the lake. It was like their secret hide-away from all their problems. Aubry opened her diary, filled with her precise hand-written script, and read through some of the entries from the past six months. She'd cost Jaxon so much and destroyed her standing in the Galactic Alliance diplomatic envoy when she'd entered into a forbidden love affair.

She'd initially come to Kashim almost a year ago as a governess for the younger royal children to educate them on the customs of the polite etiquette which all planets in the Alliance abided by. They were the future of a world that needed to put their xenophobic ways behind them. The Kashimi did not believe in the mixing of alien races but had no choice when they joined the Galactic Alliance of Planets. They wanted a secure future for their people.

Aubry peered through the triangular window at her still-sleeping fiancé. His coarse, white hair stuck out in every direction. He was growing it longer now that he'd completed his flight combat training. Jaxon was away when she first arrived on Kashim. When he returned several months later, she was absolutely smitten seeing him in his military attire for the first time. Aubry never believed in love at first sight until that moment. She couldn't believe he felt the same way when he'd asked her to dance at a formal engagement celebration for one of his brothers.

It was a magical night. Aubry felt like they were floating on air as they glided around the beautifully decorated courtyard beneath glowing golden lanterns. From then on, they were inseparable. He filled her soul with a warm, comforting glow when they were together. When he left to attend to his Alliance military duties, she missed him fiercely. Aubry sent him love notes every day through the satellite relay network. His messages, in return, made her heart swell. She'd been positively giddy.

The royal family begrudgingly tolerated their affair as a casual fling to help better the Kashim's rela-tionship with the Alliance; a young man, sowing his wild oats. When the time came, he would do his duty and submit to an arranged, politically advantageous marriage with a proper Kashimi woman. But when a child was conceived from their union, xenophobia rose its ugly head again. They'd stripped him of the Moul al' Tesha-san royal household name and ordered him to leave Kashim for good. Jaxon planned to take her Raymonton surname when they married.

He opened his eyes and smiled when he saw her. Waving his hand, he motioned for her to come inside. "Are you sure you're okay for the climb today? I thought I heard you throwing up earlier."

"Yes. It's just normal morning sickness for a Terran. It's early enough in my pregnancy that there are no physical restrictions for me yet. I trust you'll keep us safe on the climb."

Jaxon sat up, throwing his legs over the side of the bed and stretching. "You checked the full mask to make sure it'll provide enough oxygen for you?"

"Yes. It was wonderful, like breathing Earth air."

Jaxon smiled as he dressed. "I hope to get assigned to an Alliance base near Earth one day. I'm looking forward to exploring your homeworld together with our son."

"Me too," Aubry said as she changed into her hiking gear. "Have you received word on your first deployment yet?"

"Yes. We'll be moving to Blackstar Base near Kax'ad. I'll be joining a fighter squadron there in the conflict against the Brunne."

Aubry hadn't expected to be a military wife, but

here she was about to marry a fighter pilot. She had traveled all around the galaxy in her diplomatic duties and seen many amazing worlds. Now she'd be doing it at a soldier's side as they moved from base to base while Jaxon fought in conflicts, defending Alliance territories. She hoped to get a teaching job at the base, now that she was banned from the GAP diplomatic envoy for her indiscretion.

"I'll make us a quick breakfast, and then we'll get going," he said, kissing her cheek.

Aubry breathed heavily as they scaled the mountainside. They'd spent most of the day hiking, and the outer edges of her face mask were beginning to fog up. She pressed a button on the side to activate the defogger. Fans lightly hummed as they whisked away the excess moisture. Jaxon was several steps ahead of her. His rigorous military training had prepared him well for the steep climb. A heavy cloud layer loomed ahead. He climbed higher to secure the safety lines for her. Giving her a thumbs-up sign, he disappeared into the thick, misty layer. Aubry took a deep breath and pushed forward, feeling chilled as the foggy air enveloped her. It was eerily quiet inside and a little disconcerting not being able to see the way ahead. Beads of condensation formed on her climbing suit. She continued the ascent, hand over hand, grabbing the lines tighter, fearing she'd lose her grip on the slick, damp rope. Her hand slipped away, and she grabbed for the ledge, fingers slipping on the wet surface.

Jaxon's gloved hand pierced the fog like a lifeline to grab hers and pull Aubry through the hazy layer to the top of the spire. She closed her eyes, breathing hard from the arduous climb. When she opened them, she beheld a glorious sight. The dark moon, Kamaria, loomed huge on the horizon. Lights from the Borealis colony settlement twinkled on the western hemisphere. Aubry shaded her eyes against the sun shining brightly over the moon's right shoulder. The light revealed two other spires peeking over the sea of clouds.

"Wow . . . It's incredible. I can't even put into words how beautiful it is," said Aubry, eyes wide, taking in the view before her.

"I told you it was something to behold." Jaxon laid his arm around her shoulder. "See that spire off to the left?" he said, pointing.

Aubry nodded.

"That marks the boundary between the kingdom of Moul al' Tesha-san and the ancient territory of the Pro'az Shah Ma-te. The two lands were torn apart by a long and brutal war. Princess Marza climbed this spire every day to see her love, who scaled the other spire over there. They used elaborate hand signals to communicate their devotion to each other."

"Sounds romantic," said Aubry, gazing at him.

Jaxon took a few steps away from her, straightening his body, and squaring his shoulders. He raised one hand over his head, the other held out to the side and made sweeping arcs with his arms while forming his hands into different gestures. His motions churned charged particles in the air, creating a sparkling slipstream. Each wave flowed seamlessly into the next. The movements were delicate and graceful, like a beautiful dance. He finished by bringing his arms to his waist and clasping his hands.

"That was lovely. What does it mean?"

He laid his hands on her shoulders and looked into her eyes. "You awaken my soul. My mind and heart are at peace when I gaze upon you. Our love will forever keep us together."

Aubry couldn't say anything at that moment; the words so moved her. Jaxon caressed the mask's faceplate.

"I wish I could kiss you right now."

Aubry smiled. "So how does their story end? Are the lovers finally reunited?"

Jaxon's lips curled into a slight grimace, and his shoulders slumped. "Unfortunately . . . no. Tensions increased between the two lands, and the fighting escalated. The princess threw herself from the spire when she realized she would never hold her love in her arms again. In despair, he followed suit and jumped to his death to join her in the afterworld where they could finally be reunited."

"How very Romeo and Juliet," said Aubry.

"Who're they?"

"An old Earth play. A tragedy of two rival families in conflict and two star-crossed lovers who commit suicide when they can't be together."

"It's interesting how so many cultures across the galaxy have tragic tales of doomed lovers," Jaxon said, wrapping his arms around her. Aubry stiffened a bit in his embrace.

"You know I didn't mean us, right?" he said, eyes filling with concern.

"Of course. You and the baby are my life now," she said, laying her hand on his chest, feeling his heart beat steady and strong.

Jaxon took the comm from his pocket and held it out before them to take a holovid and picture, commemorating their last day on Kashim.

"And it's going to be an amazing life. I consider it my honor and duty to love you always and will do everything in my power to make you happy. Come on, let's head down before it gets too much darker. The journey of our grand adventure together awaits."

About L.A. Stinnett

L.A. Stinnett is a writer of fanciful tales in the sci-fi and fantasy genres. My debut novel "The Blood Witch Chronicles" and the companion novella "The Last Dragon Riders of Eleanthra" released in 2020. I will be releasing my fantasy novella "Spirit of Stone" in 2021 as well as participating in several anthologies.

Find out more about L.A. Stinnett below.

Website:

https://sites.google.com/view/l-a-stinnett-fantasy-writer/

Twitter: @StinnettLa

Slow Recovery
by Ian Martínez Cassmeyer

When Juan awoke, he couldn't recall how he'd ended up in the starship medical bay. His vision was a bit unfocused, and his head throbbed. A concussion, most likely, so he didn't sit up. Another dull sting also emanated from his right arm. Slowly, he lifted it over his head, and his heartbeat broke into a sprint.

A bandage encased his whole arm below the elbow—everything but his missing forefinger and thumb. What in the galaxy had happened to him?

He was lying back in a med-bay bed, staring up at the ceiling. The light fixtures above, shining down their antiseptic glow confirmed where he was. It was much louder than he recalled—the air was full of groaning, squeals of pain, hurried footfalls, and metallic clatter.

31

That meant the med-bay was busy. But, why was the med-bay busy? And, why wasn't he helping? What had happened?

He fumbled for a moment until he found the buttons that controlled his bed and crushed the one that would bring him back to an upright position. He had to figure out what had happened, and he couldn't do that lying there like a lump of dough.

"Oh, no you don't, you stay right where you are."

The sudden stern tone in the voice caused Juan to draw back his hand from the button, as if it was a burning stove. The voice was familiar, but his mind sputtered for a moment looking for the name to which it belonged. Was his memory loss that severe? Was the trauma interfering with his cognitive processing? The urgency to get up and find answers increased.

Before he could hit the button again, someone grabbed his hand. A face entered his field of vision. It was a young woman, her sable hair pulled back in a ponytail, and her dark brown eyes staring down at him. "I said don't, Juan. Please, just relax."

The voice. The face. The two elements clicked immediately in his mind. "Julia? When did you get here?"

"About two hours ago. I've been running things in your place."

She leaned down and kissed him on the lips. For a moment, everything else in the world vanished. When things did come back into focus, so too did a few details about the journey. The *ESS Livingstone* was heading toward Perez Landing — the "Fish Bowl" as everyone called it — for a long period of leave after being out among the stars for nearly nine months.

As happy as Juan was to see his wife, questions flooded his mind again. "But…why are you here, Jules?"

The expression on her face went from subdued joy to pure concern. "You mean…you really don't remember?"

Juan shook his head. "I can't remember how I got here." He tried searching his memory, but all he found where his most recent memories should've been was a massive grey patch, like a corridor full of fog. He tried going back further — to the night before.

Yes. There he could see something concrete. He'd done all the necessary end-of-day prep he'd needed to do. One last round of in-patient check-ups; a final check up on the med-bay database and system; inventory for the medical supplies. Before the *Livingstone* could ship out again, it would need to resupply — amazing how much gauze and bandages a ship could go through in nine months.

Then he'd gone to bed.

Now he was here.

He told Julia everything between was a blank.

"All the more reason to stay in bed," Julia said. "You suffered a major head injury. Now lay back."

"No Jules. This is my med-bay, and I need to — "

The bay doors *whooshed* open. "Please do as Dr. Rosario asks, Dr. Ramos," said another familiar voice.

"We wouldn't want you to hurt yourself."

Juan turned in time to see Captain Austin Eggers walk into med-bay, a cup of coffee in each hand. When he reached the side of his bed, he held out one to Juan. Juan grabbed it with his good left hand. "Austin, I assure you, it's not as bad as it looks."

"That hand of yours says otherwise," the Captain said, taking a sip.

Juan glanced at his now tri-digited right hand. "Okay, it's pretty bad, but—"

"I insist, Doctor, that you take it easy for now. Dr. Rosario has been doing a fine job looking after things since we fought off the Nebul attack."

Nebuls? Nebuls had attacked them? Was it then that he'd gotten hurt and ended up here? Juan tried searching his memory again, but the foggy corridor of his mind revealed nothing. Maybe, though, he could illuminate and burn away some of the fog, if he asked the right questions. "Um, remind me, Captain. How far are we from Perez Landing?"

The Captain finished another sip of coffee. "We were 3 hours out before the Nebuls attacked, but now that we're moving again, we should be there in about two and a half."

Juan glanced around the room until he found the clock. It read 8 PM *EWHCST*—meaning Earth's Western Hemisphere Central Standard Time. He'd gone to bed last night at 10, like always.

"Make sure you drink that while it's hot Doctor,"

said the Captain, motioning toward Juan's untouched cup.

Assuming he'd slept his usual 8 hours, Juan had lost 14 hours of memory—that meant his was likely a case of post-traumatic amnesia. Filling that gap would take a while, but he was sure he'd gather it.

But first, coffee.

He took a quick sip of it. Dark roast—but no milk. Not his favorite way to drink it, but it would do. Coffee was a welcomed commodity this far out in space. He took a sniff of it. The fresh aromas made him want to almost get up and click his heels. Of course, he knew Julia would chastise him if he did, so he refrained.

Then Juan blinked a few times. Something was coming back to him—back out of the fog.

Morning—with no sun, precisely timed clocks determined these things—had found Juan in his usual spot: in front of the med-bay coffeepot, waiting for it to finish brewing. He could afford to take such moments, and not just because he was a freakishly early riser. The starship, *Earth Space Ship (ESS) Livingstone*, had encountered no issues on the way to the Perez Landing, so there'd been very little activity in the med-bay, besides the typical small scrapes and bruises.

The pot finished brewing, and Juan poured his first

cup. Dark roast, with a little milk, just as he preferred. He paused a moment to savor the smell, but before he could take a sip, the halo-com on his wrist buzzed.

He flicked his wrist back, and the hologram of the Captain hovered before him. "Have you had your first coffee with milk yet, Juan?"

Leave it to the Captain to know Juan's habits like the back of his hand. He held up his cup in front of the halo-com. "I was just about to when you called, Austin."

Austin chuckled. "How are things in your department?"

"Running smoothly. The staff isn't fully here yet, but they've still got plenty of time to report in."

"Good to hear, Juan. How's our medical supply holding up?"

"Funny you ask. For the most part, we're holding out okay, but we'll definitely want to restock our pharmacy, our onboard blood supply, and maybe get our equipment looked at, just in case."

Austin chuckled again. "Thorough as usual, I see."

"I do my best," said Juan. "Estimated docking time?"

"We're still about 3 hours away from the Landing."

Perez Landing—two words, which to Juan meant some much needed and much welcomed leave time. Sure it would be only for three months, but three months was three months—and it wouldn't be just any three months either.

Juan and Julia were set to celebrate their 10th anniversary there—back at the place where they'd originally met. Perez Landing, with its massive atmospheric dome that stood high above its three towering peaks. Space Corps life wasn't easy on married couples, but they'd made it work by staying in constant contact with each other during their periods of separation.

"What do you think you and Jules will do while you have the time off?" said Austin. Juan frowned at the hologram in front of him. "You've got *that look* on your face, so I know you're thinking about her."

Juan smiled. "I'm not sure yet. But we'll have plenty of time to decide."

"Well, if I could make a suggestion, what about taking a trip up Mt. Tegus?"

Juan pondered the idea for a moment as he raised his coffee to his lips. It was atop Mt. Tegus, the highest of the three peaks, where he'd asked Julia to marry him—and she'd said yes. Maybe it was time to revisit that sacred site again. "It's a good idea..."

"Well, you still have 3 hours to think it over, assuming nothing goes—"

The ship's alarm system blared with the force of a full brass band. Scarlet lights flashed through the medical bay. Then, the alarm voice spoke:

Alert. Alert. Nebul ship approaching the starboard side on attack vector.

Austin and Juan cut their connection. Attack vector meant injuries—and likely fatalities. Juan set down his coffee and went to prepare the bay.

Julia finished enclosing Juan's arm in the Axolot-Rig. His injuries had healed to the point where the limb regenerating process could begin. How long had he been in that coma? It would take longer than just surgically attaching a new cybernetic forefinger and thumb, but the result was always worth the slow recovery.

"Okay, Jules," he said. "Now, can I please—ouch!"

She'd fired up the Axolot-Rig. Juan had never experienced the jolt of its healing process beginning to work. Until now, he'd been the one strapping the appliance to other people's limbs. "Don't be such a baby, and no to whatever you were about to say."

He groaned. "Jules, please. I'm going stir-crazy here."

"Juan, your priority needs to be recovery. Besides I have things running smoothly here."

Doctor to doctor, he knew she was right, but between the blank patch in his memory and his hatred of *doing nothing* he couldn't help himself. "Jules, we were attacked. I still can't remember how I got here, and curiosity is scratching the back of my brain like a cat on a couch. I need to see what's happened, so please, let me move around...a *little*?"

Julia stared at him, her left eyebrow cocked at a skeptical angle. She sighed. "Fine...*But*, only if you go around in a hover chair."

38

Juan deflated slightly. He should've seen that one coming. The idea to muster an argument about how he *wasn't* an invalid, that it was his hand, not his *legs* that were injured, and that the hover chairs should be reserved for people who *really needed them* briefly tempted him — but with Julia, he knew it was pointless. From a medical viewpoint, after suffering a coma and amnesia-inducing concussion, there remained a likelihood that he could suddenly collapse unconscious and cause further injury to himself. So, it wasn't *unreasonable* to be cautious — but it was annoying.

Julia pushed the chair over and helped him into it. Thankfully, it was an electric medical chair, so all he'd have to do to move around was manipulate the control on the left armrest. Once he'd gotten the hang of the controls, Juan hovered around the many other beds and looked at each of the charts.

Every one of the patients had one of the rollcall of post-battle wounds: blaster shots, burns, missing limbs, shrapnel, and so on. He asked several of the medical staff for updates on the treatments. Most had administered basic triaged and pain-management, which were smart calls. Considering how close they were to the Fish Bowl, these basic measures were the best they could manage — especially due to the number of patients.

One chart of one bed he passed said its occupant was Lt. Commander Liza Bergen. Juan almost didn't recognize her from the battered bruised face peering out her heavily-bandaged head and torso. How had that happened?

One thing struck him as unusual: he saw no Nebuls in the med-bay. He hovered over to Julia. "Hey Jules, quick question."

"What?"

He motioned for her to follow him away from some of the patients. "Were there any…" he glanced around to make sure no one was in earshot, but still spoke in a whisper. "Were there any Nebul survivors?"

Julia mirrored Juan's caution. "Yes," she said. "A few. The captain ordered us to keep them in the brig."

Juan exhaled, an acute tension in his mind eased. For decades, since humanity had settled on Perez Landing, intermittent conflicts between humans and Nebuls, like this one, had happened. Many of the Nebul people believed humanity should leave the system. There were many among the *Livingstone* crew, and some residents of the Fish Bowl, who believed in the total annihilation of the Nebuls.

The two peoples, however, had reached compromise: the Nebuls would allow humanity to stay, provided they didn't expand their territory beyond the Landing. "There was no reason the two peoples couldn't coexist," the Nebul Leaders had said.

Of course, not everyone believed that, on either side. Juan, however, was of that opinion. As a medical professional, every life had value—even the lives of those who may hate you.

He glanced around the at-capacity med-bay.

Despite the carnage, at least it hadn't ended in a complete slaughter, and, however he'd ended up here, he'd gotten lucky.

"I think I'll step out and look around the ship," he said.

"Hoping something will jog the memory?"

He nodded. There was still so much fog in the corridor. He couldn't penetrate it any deeper, at least not on his own. But maybe—maybe if he saw where everything had happened, it might give him a clue. "Where did the battles happen?"

Julia told him and pointed him down the hallway from the med-bay towards the bridge. That was logical; any attacking force would always try to take command of the ship first. Capturing the Captain was like capturing the King in chess—game, set, match. Of course, Austin wouldn't have gone down without fighting.

The closer he drew to the flight deck, the more obvious the battle damage became. Onboard maintenance bots worked away, rewiring, replacing, and soldering things into place. Overseeing them were the maintenance crewmembers, chief among them Maurice. "Okay, get that slab back over there and fix it in place."

The bots did so.

"Seems like you've got a lot of work on your hands, Maury," said Juan.

"Well, well, look who's up from his nap," said Maurice, as he clomped over to him, "How you feeling Doc?"

"Still alive."

"And the folks in med-bay?"

"On the mend, but we definitely need to—"

A bright flash of sparks from the bots' soldering work made Juan flinch.

"Careful you titanium-plated dunderheads, there are people present," said Maurice. "So, anyway, Doc tell me—"

But Juan's attention was elsewhere. The sparks had illuminated another patch in the corridor.

Blaster-bolts frayed the makeshift cover the soldiers had fashioned from a warped steel slab. Each bolt showered Juan in sparks and perfumed the air with an aroma of burning metal. The Nebuls had all boarded from one ship, at one point through the burglar hole they'd cut into the side of the ship several yards down the hallway—a sneaky tactic.

However, it also left them vulnerable in one way: all their forces were in one place.

The soldiers at the bow and the soldiers at the stern had fought to keep them contained within one wide corridor, boxing them in. It was only a matter of time before they met in the middle.

The exchange had been an absolute meat-grinder.

Juan couldn't stay in the med-bay any longer in

good conscience as gurney after gurney with a wounded soldier came through. He had several medics go down and around to help the stern soldiers while he and his aides helped the bow crewmates.

"What kind of idiocy is this?" said Liza. She stood up, fired a few rounds over the junkyard parapet, and ducked. "There's no strategy. They come in one place," she stood, fired, and ducked again. "Instead of dividing our forces, they're just trying to wipe us out," — again, same sequence — "does it make sense to you, Doc?"

Juan swabbed at a fallen soldier's blaster wound. The sedative spray he'd administered earlier kept him from squiggling. Had he been fully conscious, he would've yelped like a kicked puppy — the antiseptic stung like a hornet on contact. "Honestly, Liza. What they're thinking hasn't crossed my mind." He bandaged the wounds and instructed two of his aides to get the soldier to the med-bay quickly. Another volley of blaster-bolts sent sparks cascading down. "What concerns me is what they're doing."

The line started to move forward. Juan and his remaining medics crawled behind the soldiers. If the Nebuls injured him, or any of his staffers, it would screw up the whole operation.

More volleys.

More sparks.

The air so became thick with the charred metal that Juan wrapped his face in a spare bit of cloth. The cacophony of blaster-fire drowned out the voices of the

43

commanders that they switched to their holo-coms to communicate properly. The line kept moving.

As they inched around another bit of makeshift cover, the platoon Juan and his medics followed came across a fallen Nebul soldier. Several black blaster shots, where the heat had cauterized their skin, dotted the Nebul's arm, but the wound they were nursing was their right thigh. Something had torn into their thigh. They had one blue blood-stained hand guarding the wound and lay on the ground, seething in pain.

Liza raised her gun at the Nebul, but Juan stepped between them.

"Get out of the way, Doc," she said, her gun still raised. "That's the enemy."

Juan didn't move. Even if this Nebul soldier had been shooting at them, they deserved medical treatment.

"Doctor!"

"Lieutenant, this soldier needs medical attention and I will provide it."

More volleys.

More sparks.

Liza lowered her gun and let out a sharp sigh. "Soldiers, follow me." The platoon slithered, single-file through the maze of makeshift cover ahead. One of Juan's medics followed them while his other two stayed behind with him.

He knelt next to the Nebul and raised his hands, showing he meant no harm. At first, the Nebul tried to inch away from him, guarding their wound.

Then, in the Nebul language, he said, "You're injured. I'm here to help."

The tension eased in the Nebul's body, and they nodded. Juan asked his medics for the items he'd need to begin treatment. Humans were only just beginning to understand Nebul anatomy, but their bodies in many ways were similar to those of humankind. A stroke of convergent evolutionary luck, light-years away.

The wound wasn't hemorrhaging blood, which meant there was no major vessel damage. He took out his bottle of sedative spray and spritzed the Nebul in the face. The Nebul relaxed. They leaned back, closed their eyes, and began to snooze. Juan moved their hands away and looked at the wound.

Several shrapnel shards had indeed dug into the Nebul's skin. Juan took out a set of prongs and a set of tweezers. By the time he was done, he'd removed seven pieces. He bound the wound tightly and told him medics to get the soldier back to the med-bay.

Juan crawled up the path the soldiers had followed.

More volleys.

More sparks.

Then, the blasting ceased.

Silence shrouded the battle zone like a blanket of snow. Had they exhausted all the Nebuls' ammo? Had they finally retreated? He came up behind the platoon. Liza and her soldiers squatted below the edge of another steel slab parapet. An itch made Juan want to know what was ahead, so he went around the platoon. Liza whisper-shouted at him to stay behind them, but he ventured on anyway.

A lone Nebul solider lay in the middle of a considerable open area. Juan crept closer to see if they too were injured. He was inches from the soldier when a sound pierced the silence.

Beep. Beep. Beep.

Juan turned the soldier over. Their eyes were half open and glazed over, but clutched to their chest was a belt of three metal spheres. Red lights flashed in rhythm to the beeps he had heard earlier.

Then the red lights became stable.

The *beeps* crescendoed to a loud roar.

Juan slipped over some dusty rubble behind him as he tried to retreat. His heart pounded so loud in his ears, it nearly drowned out the drone. Someone grabbed him from behind. With considerable strength, they threw him over the nearest pile of rubble.

The bombs exploded.

A harsh ring buzzed in Juan's ears. He crawled from behind to see who had saved him. On the floor, her face bloody, and her body limp was Liza. Juan shouted to his medical staff to get to the front quickly. They had to save her. No matter what, they had to save her.

The bridge door *whooshed* open when Juan approached it. Juan stopped his hover chair at the lip of the door. He wiped his eyes and tried to compose himself. So he was the one responsible for Liza's condition? If she didn't live, he didn't know how he could forgive himself. He wiped the gathering tears from his eyes and cleared his throat. "Permission to enter the bridge, Captain."

"Granted," said Austin.

A quick once-over told Juan that little fighting had happened on the bridge. A few blaster burns dotted the walls, but none of the navigation equipment or consoles looked damaged. "I see your forces earned their reputation for incredible defense, Austin."

"Indeed, Doctor," Austin stood before the main console, examining several screens. "The Nebuls never set foot on the bridge. Our pincer movement worked perfectly." He then turned toward Juan. "Good to see you up and about, Doctor. How may I help you?"

Juan didn't bother to say he wasn't quite *up* yet, but he was about certainly. "I just wanted to ask you something, Austin." He maneuvered his hover chair closer to him and spoke in a whisper. "Have any of the prisoners received further treatment?"

Austin leaned back. "Why should they? They're the enemy."

Juan resisted the urge to roll his eyes. He and Austin had been having this debate for twelve years now, and neither had managed to make any headway convincing the other. "I know how you feel about the

Nebuls, Austin, but they're still living beings and they deserve—"

"They deserve? They deserve whatever we decide they deserve for what they did."

He turned his back and mumbled something. Juan was certain of what he said: *alien scum*. A small ache panged in his chest. Austin had many admirable characteristics, but this was not one of them. Like many soldiers who've seen too many of their own die, he'd truly come to hate his enemy to the point where he couldn't recognize their personhood anymore.

Images flashed in Juan's mind. Liza's battered body in that med-bay bed. The fallen soldier he'd treated in battle. The dead Nebul, clutching the belt of bombs. Carnage. Carnage. Carnage.

He could understand Austin's sentiments—but that still didn't mean he was right.

"Austin, if you truly believe that," Juan continued. "Then why didn't you just have all the prisoners terminated?"

Austin said nothing. That's all he ever did when this topic came up between them — go as silent as the vacuum of space. Juan turned for a moment to the window at the front of the bridge. The dome of Perez Landing was now in view and growing gradually closer. It was probably best to change the subject anyway. "How far are we from the Fish Bowl?"

"*Mavis*, how long until we reach Perez Landing?" said Austin.

"Are you feeling okay, Captain? Your voice sounds off." The synthesized voice belonging to the ship's AI said.

"I'm fine *Mavis*. Just a bit worn from the fighting earlier. Please answer the previous question."

"Acknowledged," said *Mavis*, "The *Livingstone* will arrive at port in one and a half hours, Captain."

"Could you bring up a three-dimensional map of our current course?"

"Acknowledged." The room darkened, and a monochrome three-dimensional scale model of their current position in space filled the room. A scale model of the *Livingstone* crept closer through the starry gulf toward the Fish Bowl's facsimile. "As I said — we will arrive in port in one and a half hours Captain."

"Thank you, *Mavis*." The hologram vanished.

Juan turned his hover chair around. "Whether you condone it or not, I'll be asking some of the medics to help me down in the brig with prisoner treatment." Until they reached the Fish Bowl, that's all he could do. Once they landed, their care and fate would be out of Juan's hands.

"Do as you wish, Doctor," he said, wiping his mouth. He sat in his captain's chair without looking at Juan. "Do me one favor though, Doctor. Prioritize our crew's recovery...along with your own."

Juan looked down at the Axolot-Rig braced over his hand. "Will do." He headed to the bridge entrance. The door *whooshed* open again.

Hovering down the corridor, Juan couldn't shake a strange feeling that something more serious was wrong with the Captain—something he couldn't quite pinpoint. Something must've happened during the attack that caused his sudden coldness.

Why had he been so formal the whole time? Why hadn't he called him by his first name? After serving together for so long, they were always *Austin* and *Juan* no matter the circumstance or disagreement. He was missing something—but he hadn't a clue what it was.

Only 20 Nebuls remained. 20 of a crew that had to be at least 200 according to other accounts. Juan briefly wondered what the captain had ordered done with the bodies, but he figured it was better not to hypothesize.

Julia had agreed to let Juan commandeer several medics to treat the prisoners. Though, she also insisted that several more guards accompany them down in the brig. The guards down in the brig had manacled the most able-bodied Nebuls to the med-beds, all of which the *Livingstone* had commandeered from the *Arco*, Julia's ship.

Going from one bed to the next, Juan examined each of the Nebuls. Some of their wounds were superficial—a blaster shot here and there. Some of them, however, were badly injured; the medics had thought it best to place them in medically induced comas. Their bodies had incurred multiple blaster injuries, had numerous shrapnel shards lodged into them, or were now missing limbs.

Juan had the medics change the bandages of every one who needed it. For those in the comas, he checked vitals and had them rig up fresh IV fluids and medications — hard to do with only one fully functional hand — where necessary. For some this was not a problem, but Juan also noticed the scowls some of his colleagues worn when approaching the Nebuls. They approached them the same way one might approach an unfamiliar animal.

Juan refrained from remarking on the issue. Instead, he hovered over to the next bed and the next patient. With his mental corridor still foggy, it was better for him to work. At least, it would serve some purpose.

"So, what do we have here?" he said.

The medic, one of Julia's staff, stood there chart in hand. "Surface wounds," she said. "Nothing serious. Whoever treated this one last must've given them a strong sedative. They've been asleep for hours."

Their body was probably recovering from the trauma of battle that way. Juan had seen such reactions in people, but never in a Nebul. He maneuvered his chair over to the side of the bed to take their pulse. Nebuls had no veins in their wrist, but they did have several large ones in their necks, which were ideal for checking vitals.

Juan placed two fingers on the Nebul's neck.

Suddenly, the Nebul's eyes opened. They grabbed Juan by the wrist and sprung from the bed. They twisted his arm behind his head and dragged Juan, hover chair and all, towards the middle of the room.

The guards immediately charged in, blasters poised to fire. Juan told them to lower their weapons. Of course, they didn't.

A rattle of metal followed, and Juan felt a sharp point poke into the side of his neck. A table full of metal medical implements stood near enough for him to notice it from the corner of his eye. Though he couldn't see it, if he had to guess, the Nebul had a scalpel aimed at his throat.

"Lower the blade," said one of the guards. "Drop it, now."

The Nebul shouted back in their language— repeating the same three word phrase. "Let us go."

The guards only kept shouting. Likely, none of them could speak Nebul, and Juan was unsure if the Nebul could understand their language. It was a true example of a failure to communicate. The angrier the Nebul got with the guards, the harder they forced the blade into his neck and tightened the grip on his arm.

The blade-tip pierced Juan's skin.

A trickle of warmth coursed down his neck. If he didn't do something, he was dead. Juan searched his memory for the words. Thankfully, that part of his mind was perfectly clear. "Please," he said, in Nebul. "Don't do this."

The shouting stopped.

There was a *spritz*. A strange perfume stung at Juan's nostrils. Chemical, yet familiar.

Then Juan's captor collapsed over his shoulders. The suddenness caused the weight of the hover chair to shift. The chair tilted to one side, and both of them collapsed to the floor. Juan managed to break his fall with his good arm, but landing on metal still smarted.

Two guards rushed around him, along with two medics. Juan shifted to look behind him. The medics immediately lifted his former captor and carried them back to their bed. The guards however, now had in hand a surprise: another Nebul, holding a spray bottle of anesthetic.

The Nebul locked eyes with Juan and nodded.

Juan gave the Nebul a quick once over. The only apparent wounds were a bandaged arm and leg. A smirk crawled across his face when he recognized the Nebul he'd treated mid-battle earlier that day. He nodded back.

One of the guards escorted his savior back to their bunk. The other came over, anesthetic in hand, and helped him up. He then righted the hover chair, and Juan sat back down.

The guard held the bottle out to Juan. "Lucky turn of events, huh Doctor?"

Juan didn't reply. He looked at the bottle closely. His attention again shifted inward.

Two demolitionists strapped about a dozen incendiary devices to the door. Wired together with them were an equal number of smoke bombs. This combination would both destroy the barricade then provide initial cover for the first wave of the charge.

Juan and his medical staff stayed back, while Austin stood directly before the door, his helmet under his arm, ready to charge in with the first wave of men. Once the bombs were ready, he turned to his nearest officer — the communication specialist. The officer tapped a few times on his hacker-pad before turning to the Captain and nodded.

Austin then clicked his halo-com and raised it to his mouth. "Attention, Nebul Intruders, this is Captain Austin Eggers of the *ESS Livingstone* speaking. As Commanding Officer of this vessel, and a representative of humankind, I am demanding that you cease your foolhardy invasion and surrender. If you do, we'll be merciful. If, however, you continue this course, it will only lead to your absolute demise." He lowered his halo-com.

His claim of mercy was sincere. Austin may have harbored a deep hatred of the Nebuls, but once he made a promise, he kept it.

Juan held his breath for several moments. More than anything, he wished for the Nebuls to surrender.

There couldn't be that many of them left, so why not surrender and live? What had been the point of this attack in the first place? A force of no more than 200 attacking a ship like the *Livingstone* — it was madness.

Silence draped the scene like a sudden stilled breeze.

Austin turned to the demolitionists. "Blow it." He put on his helmet — the wordless signal to all the solider to ready themselves.

Juan and his staff readied themselves. How many bodies would fall after this?

One demolitionist handed Austin a remote. He lifted his other hand over his head, three fingers extended. Slowly, he counted down the moment.

Three.

Two.

One.

A concussive explosion *banged* through the air, and the whole corridor filled with white smoke. Visibility immediately dropped to nearly nothing, but the sounds of firing blaster bolts scattered through the air. Yelps of pain followed.

Juan signaled his staffers to proceed with extreme caution and stay close to the ground. If any of their soldiers had fallen, they'd be on the ground wincing in pain. One by one, they dragged their fallen and wounded crewmembers from the scene and administered triage.

The shots died down, along with the sound of

bodies falling to the floor. Juan ventured closer toward the epicenter, despite the still thick smoke. The bodies of Nebuls littered the floor besides several of their fallen comrades.

Then the silhouettes of several standing figures, huddled together in a ring came into view. They loomed over several more figures, hunched and sitting on the ground. Juan drew closer and the view cleared. Space Corps soldiers stood in a circle and the last of the Nebuls sat within it—surrounded and surrendered.

One of the taller silhouettes broke away from the ring and approached him.

"Austin?" Juan said, trepidation in his voice. "Is that you?"

"Yes, Juan, it's me. Are you okay?"

"Could be worse off," he said. "Did you capture—?"

"I think—"

Something spherical flew between them. It bounced off the wall with a metallic *clang* before rolling towards them. Then the noise started.

Beep. Beep. Beep.

Quickly, Juan ducked down, picked up the bomb, and threw it back to where it came. As it left his hand, the *beeps* crescendoed to a roar.

The bomb exploded.

Juan must've blacked out for a moment when the concussion wave broke through the air because he couldn't remember how he ended up collapsed against the wall. His body ached all over, especially his head. A searing pain emitted from his hand. He peered through the smoke, his vision blurring in and out of focus. Even in the white shroud, the red of his bloody hand stood out.

His thumb and forefinger — gone.

His heart beat faster, which only worsened the throb in his head.

A shadow loomed over him. Through his blurring gaze, he looked up. A backlit figure, whose face he could not distinguish, then bent down to him and took something from the medical bag slung over his shoulder.

Juan blinked a few times until his vision finally cleared.

The face — it was Austin's, and it wore a smile on it. Questions started rushing through his head. How was Austin not hurt? There wasn't a wound on him, yet he'd been as close to the epicenter as he'd been. The Captain placed a hand on his shoulder. "Thank you, Doctor. I couldn't have done this without you." He lifted a bottle — one full of anesthetic gas — and sprayed it.

Everything blurred, like a com-screen with no signal, and went black.

"Doctor? *Doctor*? Are you okay?" The guard said.

Juan heard his words, but he didn't respond. He was too preoccupied with what his memory had conjured up. There was no way it could be true—the Captain couldn't have done that. His mind swam with possibilities.

Suddenly things began to click together like segments of a puzzle. Austin's even more strident aloofness over their differences; that he stayed so formal most of the time, never calling him by his first name; that he hadn't brought his usual cup of coffee when he'd come to see him, which he knew by heart.

Juan ran his hand through his hair. Only one thing made sense.

Yet, simultaneously, it didn't make sense because it couldn't be true. At least, it couldn't without some confirmation.

He looked over at the Nebul he'd treated in the midst of the fight. Perhaps they'd be open to a little conversation. He told the guard that he would be fine and told him to return to his duties. He maneuvered his hover chair over to the bedside of the Nebul with the wounded leg.

He sat the spray bottle on their bedside table. "Thank you," he said in the Nebul language. "Very clever of you to think of that."

The Nebul smiled and said, "I wouldn't have remembered without you."

"You speak human language." Juan wasn't surprised. Since the Fish Bowl's founding, many humans and Nebuls had learned each other's tongues. "How has *my* accent been?"

"Not bad. A bit nasally, but not bad."

They spoke to one another for several moments. The Nebul said their "human name" — Nebuls had taken to doing this after the settlement since many humans couldn't pronounce their birth names — was Alex. They'd lived in the Fish Bowl for a large portion of their life, before enlisting in the Nebul army. Several years back, the Nebul leadership had discharged their whole platoon early once the Nebuls and Humankind had begun their alliance.

Juan had to be careful how he worded his next question. He needed an answer, but it also needed to keep from insulting his new acquaintance. "Tell me, Alex. Why are you and your compatriots here?"

Alex stared down at their injured leg. "I can't speak for us all, but I can speak for myself." They petted the wound. "Frustration. I wanted to send a message."

"What message?"

"That I mattered. That soldiers like me mattered. We weren't redundancies. We were people, and we were here. And that humans—"

"Wouldn't replace you?" said Juan.

Alex said nothing, just bowed their head. Juan only nodded and looked around. He could understand Alex's problem. The alliance had thrown their life into turmoil, cost them their livelihood. The feelings of the other 19 Nebuls likely all came from a similar wellspring—a sense of being dispossessed. But, clearly unlike Alex, something had radicalized their resentments into full-blown hatred towards humanity.

"Alex, I need you to tell me about your group's plan. What was the endgame?"

Alex said nothing for several moments. Juan could almost see the scales behind their eyes weighing the factors in the decision they were about to make. "Before we set out to do this," they said. "Our leader told us that all humans were the enemy. That your people deserved annihilation," they looked at Juan. "But, I know that's not true. You reminded me of that."

"It was the decent thing to do."

Alex nodded. "Before I tell you, let me show you something. Give you your hand."

Juan held out his intact left hand to Alex. Alex rested their left hand atop it. The skin of the hand bubbled and morphed. The beige skin darkened to a deeper brown. The fingers shortened slightly. Short black hairs sprang from the knuckles.

Then everything settled. Juan's eyes widened in both surprise and slight horror. The two hands were identical, which meant only one thing: his outlandish theory about the Captain had been right; he was a fraud.

The site of the last battle, aptly, looked like a warzone. Maurice and his crew of bots must've not made it to this section of the ship yet.

The one good thing was that the medical staff had cleared away all the fallen bodies. Juan made a mental note to thank Julia for making that sound call. However, according to what Alex had to him, there had to be one that was missing: the Captain's body.

"If we couldn't take the ship," they'd said. "Then the contingency was to take control of the ship by impersonating one of the commanding officers...preferably the Captain."

"And then what?"

"Use the ship to attack the Fish Bowl."

No one would anticipate it, especially if someone like Austin did something like that. So long as he still acted as normal as possible in public. At that moment, he was on the bridge, walking around, making sure people saw him. Why? To ward off any suspicion that he might not be who he was.

Nothing outside of the barricade doors looked suspicious. The next best place was the check the inside the storage space.

Charred marks where blaster fire had landed riddled the walls and floor. One had clearly blown out the lone light fixture, which limply dangled from the ceiling by a few wires. The air still carried a faint residue of the smoke from the bombs. The air circulation system grumbled online.

Then another scent caught Juan's attention.

It was more potent than the lingering smoke. Juan sniffed around, trying to find its source. Something about the smell made him cringe. He searched his mind for the word to describe it. Juan sniffed around a little more until he fixed on a nearby air vent.

The word came to him: putrid.

Something was indeed askew about the vent cover. It hung on the wall at the slightest crooked angle. He maneuvered the hover chair closer and realized why: one of the four screws was missing.

He jiggled the vent a little first. All three of the other screws were looser. With his one functional hand, he undid the others. It was slow and painful, but he managed to get them undone. The vent toppled backwards and clattered to the floor.

A gust of the smell struck Juan's nostrils. Tears filled his eyes, his stomach lurched, and he gagged. In the dim light inside the room, he could make out a vague outline of something inside the vent.

It looked like a foot.

Juan hovered back to the storage doors to get some air and allow his stomach to settle. Why was this so hard? As a doctor, he'd dealt with expired bodies his whole life in one way or another. This time though it was different. Doctors never handled personal cases exactly for things like this: any objective veneer crumbled before reality.

He took one more deep breath and hovered back to the vent. He grabbed the nearest bit of the figure inside and reversed the hover chair.

Captain Austin Egger's naked, lifeless body lay

on the ground. The bomb had only lightly damaged the right side of his face, as the few red spots where shrapnel had landed indicated. That helmet he'd worn had saved him. Undoubtedly though, the concussive wave that followed had knocked him out, just as it had Juan. That had left him vulnerable to what really killed him: two cauterized blaster wounds to his chest.

"Whose job was it to carry out the contingency?" Juan had asked.

"The leader of our group. He goes by the name Aaron," said Alex.

Aaron must've seen Austin incapacitated, recognized the opportunity, and took it.

Juan's chest burned. His face grew hot. Several violent thoughts passed through his mind. His breath grew short and shallow. All he wanted to do was storm the bridge and kill the man who wore his friend's face. He balled his hand into a fist so tight it hurt. He wanted to take from him what he'd taken from Austin: a future. He gritted his teeth. Had this been how Austin had felt every time he'd seen the soldiers under his command slain in battle?

Juan took another deep breath and unclenched his fist. Even if he did all that, it wouldn't bring Austin back. Out of the medical bag in his lap, Juan drew a blanket and laid it over Austin's lifeless frame.

The alert voice sounded again:

Attention all crewmembers. The ESS Livingstone will dock at Perez Landing in 15 minutes. All those intending to disembark, please prepare to do so.

They'd had their disagreements over the years, yes — disagreements that, now, they'd never be able to resolve. But, he was still his friend — and his friend deserved justice. He flicked his wrist back. A hologram of Julia flickered from his halo-com.

"Juan, where are you?"

"I'm in the warzone area, Jules." He continued before she could ask why. "Jules, I have some bad news."

Juan, Julia, and his fellow senior crewmembers followed the false Captain aboard the satellite docking station. This was the final checkpoint before the crew could head to the Fish Bowl. Every ship, Space Corps or civilian, wishing to enter Perez Landing had to stop here first.

The Captain walked up to the counter to begin processing. As he stood there, speaking to the officials, Juan exchanged glances with each of his fellow senior officers. They all knew what he was about to do and each gave their nod for him to proceed.

The last person he looked at was Julia. She had a nervous frown on her face. The truth hadn't been easy for her to hear, but seeing Austin's body was all the proof she needed to believe him. Although she hadn't liked his plan, she had agreed to it.

She took Juan's hand in hers and squeezed it. That

was their silent way of reassuring one another. He squeezed back.

Juan hovered towards the false Captain and parked himself next to him.

"Doctor," said the Captain. "How is your recovery going?"

"It's slow, of course, but progressing," said Juan, keeping his tone calm. "But my memory is doing much better."

It was subtle, but when he said those words, the impersonator leaned slightly away from him; he clearly wanted more space between them. "Your memory?" he said, his voice composed, but with a dull edge to it. "I hadn't realized it had been giving you trouble."

"Oh, yes. A bad blow," Juan lightly tapped his head with his knuckle. "From the bomb at the last skirmish with the Nebuls. You remember that, don't you?"

The impersonator shifted slightly. "Of course I do. It was a foolhardy thing to do."

"Indeed. Strange though how I ended up so banged up, and yet Julia," he pointed at her. "Tells me that you never received any kind of treatment for injuries. Seems a little odd that you'd end up perfectly fine while I," he motioned at the Axolot-Rig strapped to his hand, "ended up with this."

"Lucky, I guess." His tone grew stiffer.

"I suppose." He had no choice. He'd have to force it out of him. "You know, I just remembered that, after the explosion happened, you said something odd to me before I passed out. Do you remember?"

The impersonator's hand moved towards the blaster in his holster. "No...I don't...What did I say?"

"I think it was something like ...*Thank you, Doctor.*" The impersonator undid the clasp on his holster to keep the blaster in place. "*I couldn't have done this without you.*" He gripped the blaster, but did not draw it. "What did you mean by that?"

The impersonator didn't draw the blaster. At least, not then. He scanned around the room—he was looking for a means of escape and wasn't finding one. He fixed his gaze back on Juan. "I will say this much, Doctor," he said, his voice low so as not to draw attention. "You're quite clever."

"It's a prerequisite for the profession," Juan replied, matching his interlocutor's volume. "Everyone on the ship knows about you, Aaron—that is the name you go by, correct?"

Aaron nodded. "So, what now?"

Juan raised his arms. "I'm unarmed, and I'm not exactly highly mobile. The next move is yours. From where I sit, you have two options: surrender and end this peacefully, or shoot me and end up arrested anyway. Either way, your *mission* will fail."

Aaron said nothing, but he also didn't draw out the blaster. Perhaps there was still a chance to reason with him. "Think about this, Aaron. You began this mission with 200 of your people. With you, there are 21 of you left. And the number of humans killed and hurt because of this…we're not even sure yet." He nudged the control of the hover-chair forward and inched closer. "You have a chance to end this without violence. Why not do that?"

He held out his hand.

Aaron glanced at it. He reached out with his own and clasped Juan's hand. They shook for a moment. Then the grip tightened to a vice. Aaron hauled him forward, drew out the blaster in a flash, and the muzzle flashed.

A ring hummed in Juan's ear. He clutched the right side of his stomach. The hover chair tipped, and he collapsed to the floor. The vibrations of footfalls rumbled. Muffled shouted words rippled the air. Someone patted Juan on his shoulder.

"Juan? *Juan?*" said Julia, as she turned him over on his back. "Are you okay?"

He looked down at his shirt. The blaster had scorched through his it, but the bolt hadn't penetrated the blaster-resistant armor vest he'd put on beneath it earlier. The site stung, but he would live.

He gazed at Aaron, who was now pinned to the ground. His façade was gone, so he again resembled an untransformed Nebul. A grimaced of rage twisted his face. Juan closed his eyes and shook his head. The last question he asked Alex came back to him. "Do you think Aaron will just give up on the mission?"

"I doubt it," Alex had said. "The anger he has against humans isn't just going to go away. There are no quick solutions for these things."

About Ian Martinez Cassmeyer

Ian Martinez Cassmeyer's work has appeared on *Tor. com* and *Every Writer's Resource*, and in the anthologies *Beneath the Twin Suns*, *The New Normal*, and *In the Red Room*. He earned his B.A. at the University of Missouri-St. Louis and further studied at the James Gunn Center for the Study of Science Fiction Writing Workshop in Lawrence, Kansas. He reads slush for James Gunn's Ad Astra, maintains a blog Two Cents, and hosts 4 Cents A Podcast. Other jobs he's held include landscaper, deli clerk, and accountant assistant.

Find out more about Ian Martínez Cassmeyer below.

Website: ianstwocents.blogspot.com

Twitter: @Ian_SMC

Ascension
by Nikki Mitchell

My mother named me after the black flakes that fell from the sky when we were finally able to vanquish our long-standing enemy, the Loctari. They had come a hundred years before and enslaved our people, forcing us to dig further and further into Terra and deplete our natural caches of oil. My mother lost my father in one of the accidents that so frequently befell the oilers when the Loctari pushed them to go faster. Ever faster. She wept for the unnecessary cruelty and grief our people were subjected to, but praised the moons for allowing my father to leave her one last gift: me.

Just before the eighth month of her pregnancy, the other rebel leaders arose from their hidden tunnels and cracked the surface of Terra with a massive ship that leapt into the sky and shot for the Loctari's orbiting base. Unable to create weapons to combat the Loctari's own, they had created *Liberty* to be the weapon itself. Four of our now-international heroes manned *Liberty* on its suicide mission, flying directly into the heart of the base — the only chance we would have.

My mother described a sobering scene; one moment the base and *Liberty* were two discrete objects in the sky, our two moons casting their pale light upon Terra, and the stars winking down on us from their perches light-years away. The next moment, a bright flash replaced the base and ash began raining down. The mission was a success.

As the ash continued to fall for nine more days, the rebels poured from Terra's underground equipped with masks and homemade energy blasters. With the Loctari cut off from their base and armories, it was easy work ridding them of our lands completely. I was born early a week later. My mother claimed that I could not wait to finally taste freedom for myself.

Since the time of my birth, our moons have been blocked from our view — the ash had created an ecological shift in Terra's atmosphere and a cover of gray clouds hung evermore in the sky. I had never seen our moons, nor would ever glimpse the twinkling curiosity of the stars. Only those that were chosen to man spacecraft or colonize the worlds upon our moons were ever given the chance. I, with my heart, would never be chosen.

But I was content to remain upon Terra's surface

forever if that meant I could be wrapped in Rian's arms each night.

I gazed down at her slumbering form. As always, the sheets were pulled taught and twisted around her body, her dark hair tangled and splayed across both our pillows. She'd never been a peaceful sleeper. No, the first time we had spent the night together, I had thought she was attacking me. She had awoken that first night to me safe on the couch, a lone pillow providing warmth as my curled body tried to burrow into the cushions. Apparently, she had vivid dreams and her body did not properly paralyze itself during her REM sleep. It was not an uncommon occurrence for those who were born after the Liberation.

Eventually, we learned to adapt. In this case, we simply bought a larger bed and two sets of blankets when we merged our households.

Tenderly, I stroked a lock of curled hair away from her eyes. Although her sleep was ever anything but restful, she radiated happiness. I could feel it washing off of her. We held a simple life; one of working and living modestly, but it was a happy one.

"Ashina…" Rian murmured, sleep thick in her voice.

I slid down the bed, gently tugging a corner of the sheet from under her body and laying it upon my own. "Good morning, my darling," I replied, snuggling my face into her lavender-tinted hair.

Cracking an eye open, she used her arm to swipe

the hair from her face and kissed me before beginning the process of untangling herself from the sheets. "What time is it?"

"A little after eight. We still have plenty of time before we need to be at the Archives."

Rian and I both worked as scribes in the dusty library where our entire written history was housed. We were tasked with translating what was left of the Loctari documents as well as compiling an accurate timeline of our own history. It was tedious work, but fulfilling. When the Loctari had enslaved our people, one of the first things they had done was destroy our libraries. Most of our written documents had gone to the flame. Even now, two decades later, we were still piecing together who we were as a people—and how the Loctari had found us.

Finally freeing herself from the strangling bedclothes, she hopped out of bed, energy coursing through her lithe muscles. I couldn't help but stare. Although we were never "intimate" in the way that most meant the word, our intimacy nevertheless was strong. We simply showed our love and affection— and yes, aesthetic attraction—to each other in different ways. One of mine was to drink her beauty with my eyes, adoring the way her dark hair sat wildly atop her head, barely brushing her shoulders. The way her bare skin slightly glowed a pale green. She glanced over her shoulder at me, a grin lighting her eyes as she began to dress.

Already dressed myself, I slid out of the bed and made my way over to her for a quick hug I couldn't resist.

"What would you like for breakfast?" I asked, enjoying the squeeze of our bodies.

She pecked me on the cheek and replied, "Eggs?"

"You got it," I said as I made my way over to the kitchen.

In a few moments, I had keyed in the order for eggs over-easy, two slices of toast, and a single order of pancakes. Moving to the cupboard as Chef worked on our order, I got out the syrup we tapped ourselves from the maple trees behind the house. Just as Rian strolled in, Chef beeped.

"Great timing," she complimented as she walked by, trailing her fingers along my back.

"I have perfected the art of being a housewife," I smiled as I opened Chef's metal doors and removed two plates with steaming food piled atop.

"A housewife?" Rian asked as she accepted her egg plate. "You didn't marry the house while I was sleeping, did you? Because I might have a slight objection."

I snorted, spewing a bit of pancake. "No," I said. "It was an occupation Before. I found a document in the Archives that talked about how a part of it was cooking meals for loved ones."

"Ah, good. I would not have stood for you being the wife of another." Her face and tone were serious, but she flung a bit of egg to show her humor.

73

Ducking, I reached out to squeeze her hand. "You know you are my only."

"As you are mine," she replied, her brilliant smile creasing the skin around her eyes.

We finished our breakfast in loving silence, our fingers entwined and our lifeblood pulsing against the other's.

A boom broke our silence, coupled with the shaking of earth and house, sending small pellets of plaster down upon our heads. Brushing a white speck from Rian's hair, I asked, "What was that?"

Her eyes wide, she shook her head. "I've no idea." The next moment, she was up and stomping into her boots by the door. "Let's find out!"

I followed more slowly, not quite ready to face the change that I knew in my bones had happened. I could feel that it was something big. Something that would alter life on Terra forever.

I strode out our front door into the eternally over-cast outdoors and slipped an arm around Rian's waist where she had stopped, just feet from the doorstep. I followed her gaze, where just a few miles away, we could see curling smoke winding its way into the clouds.

"A fire?" I ventured.

"Yeah, maybe," she replied, not quite convinced. "But why would that have vibrated the ground so?"

"Perhaps an explosion, then, that resulted in fire," I replied.

She turned to me and gave an assuring smile. "That

must have been w — "

Rian cut off as a black shape appeared from the clouds and plummeted to Terra, vibrating our house and the very dirt beneath our feet even more than before as it struck the ground. It was closer than the first and a large plume of smoke almost immediately unraveled before our eyes.

Rian and I faced one another, our terror and confusion mirrored in the other's wide eyes. We pressed our bodies together, holding on with finality, neither wanting to let go for even a second. A few moments later, the sky opened as more dark shapes flew from the clouds toward Terra. Some were larger than others, but all had the capacity to kill us with the correct landing site.

We stood, transfixed, as dark shape after dark shape sliced into the ground and stuck, throwing rocks, rubble, and whatever else had previously stood there up into the air. I tried to discern some sort of pattern to the attacks, but my efforts were fruitless. The shapes seemed to be random in size and location — at least from my limited perspective. It was difficult to gather accurate data when we could not see beyond the clouds above. We had no idea what those shapes were, nor why they were hurtling down upon us.

As a chunk the size of a toddler landed a mere mile from our location and sent up a cloud of dust and debris with twice as wide a diameter, I was finally able to move my feet.

"Come on!" I tugged Rian's arm and hauled her back into our home. A roof would not offer us much protection, but it was better than being out in the open. For her part, Rian followed without complaint. As the elder in the relationship by a couple years, custom dictated I held the authority. I would be the one to keep us safe. I had solidified that promise years ago on our wedding day. Now, it looked like the moons were testing that loyalty.

I sent my mind back to the stories my mother had told me of the Loctari. Surely, there was something useful in the survival tactics she had forced me to practice over and over again until my form was perfect, my thoughts precise, and my actions calculated. I had the survival instincts pounded into me as a babe—I had only to tap into that resource to keep us safe.

Pausing in our kitchen, I closed my eyes. I breathed in through my nose for the count of ten, allowing my anxiety, fear, and insecurities to overwhelm my senses in those ten eternal moments. I could feel my heart racing as my shaking hands wrapped around my head and my breath threatened to choke me. Just before I lost all sense, I forced them all out with my seven-count exhale. My mind lay clear. Fears may have cloaked my body, but none would enter the cold fortress of my mind. I had one purpose: get Rian and myself to safety.

I opened my eyes, hands relaxing at my sides, no longer shaking. Rian stared at me with red-rimmed eyes, the healthy glow of her effervescent skin muted. I took her head in my hands, gently wiping away the salt of her dried tears from her cheeks. "It's all going to be okay," I whispered, our foreheads touching as I gazed into her amber eyes. "I've got you."

I kissed her then, pouring all of the confidence and love from my body into hers. I would keep her safe. I'd promised my life to it. I could feel her melting into my embrace, her subtle trembling beginning to subside as I curled a hand into her hair and another drawing a tattoo of safety upon her back. As her hold on me gently loosened, I allowed us to separate, taking one last long look into her eyes before I snapped into efficiency mode. Calm, cool, and collected was what those Before called it.

"Okay," I whispered to her, now holding just her hands. "I need you to go pack a bag. Grab a couple worksuits for the both of us with an extra pair of socks, and meet me back here with your terrain boots on." I gave her a squeeze, and then nudged her toward our bedroom. She broke our gaze reluctantly and hurried to do just that.

I ran to the cellar, where we kept our field equipment. A job in the Archives was not all dusty book reading and translating; sometimes we had to unearth relics from Terra itself. We kept all of our tools — including shovels of varying sizes, rope, and even life-support materials as some caves could be cut off from necessary oxygen — close at hand for we never knew when a need would arise. Now, I praised our work-oriented personalities and began to pack my own bag.

I stomped into the kitchen, still pulling on my boots when a particularly large boom knocked me off my feet. We had been hearing — and feeling — the strange objects periodically hitting Terra since we'd come inside, but this seemed to be the closest yet. In fact, I could feel the house begin to destabilize.

"Rian!" I cried out. "We have to go!"

As I picked myself off of our painstakingly-cleaned floor, now littered with plaster and bits of ceramic where our coffee mugs had fallen and shattered, I heard her footsteps running toward me.

"I'm ready!" she yelled, rushing into the kitchen. She held her boots by their laces, one sock half on and the other still in her hand. Her pack was securely fastened on her back.

"Hurry, put those on and lace them up tightly," I said as I moved to Chef and began pressing buttons. In moments, her shoes were on and water bottles and meal bars weighed down both of our packs. We looked at each other, glanced around the kitchen we'd created together, and walked out our front door, hand in hand.

The world before us was utter chaos. Our ever-gray sky was now a dark orange, reflecting Terra burning around us. Black shapes littered the ground as far as we could see, some almost standing straight up from their impact with the earth. Buildings, monuments, hovers... most were decimated from the vibrations and collision of the unknown objects, and still more groaned and collapsed even as we watched. But the worst was the bodies. Our people had not been spared in this destruction of our world, and they lay sprawled every which way. I cradled Rian's hand in my own as I felt her anguish roll off her in waves.

"Come," I said, pulling her toward one of the largest dark objects near us.

Rian stumbled along beside me, head down as she tried not to take in the images before her. My training held as my mind remained clear of the emotion that would otherwise overwhelm me. My mother had taught me that the key to survival was to act without emotion. Without any thought but for your purpose. It was what allowed The Four to sacrifice themselves and destroy the Loctari.

It was what would save Rian and I, now.

As we reached the object, I followed its height with my eyes to where it punctured the cloud cover and possibly continued even higher. This would do.

Rian paused with me as I took stock of the object before us. It looked to be made of some kind of dark rock, small hills and valleys marring its surface, but smoothened like brain tissue. Almost polished. And *moons*, it was hot! I could feel the heat emanating from it as if I had opened Chef's doors too early while he was still creating dinner.

"Ash…" Rian began, but cut off as I shrugged my bag from my shoulders and began taking out tools.

I didn't pause my unloading and sorting of the

contents of my bag as I said, "We need to put on the worksuits."

"What are we going to do?" she asked as she dropped her own bag and took out the suits.

"Climb it," I said, handing her a pair of work gloves and a rock pick.

She stopped then and straightened, letting the gloves and pick fall to the ground.

"Moons, Ash, why would we do that?"

I straightened myself, and looked into her eyes. "Whatever these rocks are, they're not stopping their assault on us." I waved around at the destruction surrounding us. Every few minutes or so, another dark shape careened from the clouds and struck Terra, sending a shocking vibration through our feet. Fires raged everywhere. People in the distance ran amok, but for the half-mile or so around us, it was deathly quiet. We had a small neighborhood, but now it seemed *too* small. As if we were the only ones left.

I could feel Rian restricting herself to continue gazing into my eyes, forcefully not looking around at the carnage.

"We have to see what's happening up there, and the only way I can think of is to climb one of these and break above the clouds."

A flicker crossed Rian's features, and she finally broke my gaze and began unfolding one of the suits. "You always were the smart one," she said, the ghost of a smile shading her words.

In silence, we dressed in the worksuits, a jump-suit composed of a blend of different fibers, designed to withstand heavy stretching and scraping without breaking down. It was perfect for exploring caves or even traveling to one of our two moons, as the material protected the wearer from almost all external forces. Whether that be sharp rocks or varying atmospheres.

We donned the gloves from my pack, then goggles, and finally hefted our rock picks as we slid our noticeably lighter packs to our respective shoulders.

Rian hefted the rock pick toward the black rock and looked at me. "How did you know?"

"I didn't," I shrugged. "I had just hoped that whatever material these were, our picks would go through it. Man-made or natural."

"It seems to be natural, from what I can tell," she replied, running her gloved hand over the rock's surface, the heat soaking into the glove and vanishing before her hand became warmer than it would sitting on top of a hover's engine.

"Well, let's see what else we can learn from the top," I said, knowing that the longer we remained, the higher our chances were of getting hit by another rock or debris. Or swallowed by the fires closing in.

We climbed in silence, punctuated only by the continual boom of another black rock hitting Terra. At those moments, we paused our ascent as we clung to the face of our own black rock, our rock picks and the toes of our boots wedged in its sulci. Although this rock wasn't as steep as others I had dismissed for just that reason, it was still likely greater than fifty degrees from Terra's surface.

Near the beginning of our climb, we had talked to keep our minds from what was happening below us, and we had agreed that this rock must have come from outside of Terra's orbit, passing through our atmosphere to gain such a polished surface. Which also would explain the heat our worksuits continuously absorbed. But as more moments passed, our energy gradually waned and we had had to save our breathing about half a mile ago.

A mile later into our climb, we stopped to rest and eat. The dropping black rocks had become more and more infrequent, but by then the fire had completely circled our rock. From our vantage, we could see that it stretched for miles, and was expanding outward now that it had exhausted everything within its circle.

"Our home," Rian whispered in a broken voice, her shoulders slumped forward as she sat upon the rock. I followed her gaze and took in the red roof that had sat upon our house. Now, it sagged on the ground, all beneath it swallowed by the orange and red flames.

I crawled to Rian and stuck our picks into a groove at our feet so that we wouldn't slide. And then we held each other for an eternity, our tears dripping to sizzle on the black rock beneath us.

It was impossible to tell how long we had gripped the other, breathing in her scent and reminding ourselves that we were safe. We were together. But at some later point, we broke apart, uncurling our bodies from the S as we'd lain on the rock. I took out the water and meal bars, never allowing Rian's hands to leave my body. The clearness that had opened my mind on the ground was now gone. Instead, it was replaced by hollow grief.

We ate in silence, our bodies ever touching as we gazed upon the fire that had been our world. We could see nothing now, but the flames.

As the meal bars infused our exhausted muscles and minds with energy, we packed up and began anew our climb.

We continued in that routine for days, perhaps weeks. We were never wanting for water as our water bottles refilled themselves from the atmosphere around us on command, and I had grabbed enough meal bars to hopefully last months. The bars were imbued with a composition of different chemicals, intended to enhance our mortal bodies and allow us heightened abilities, including speed and endurance. Having never tried the bars ourselves before, we were not sure how often we were required to eat. We simply waited until the pang of hunger sat upon us. But with no way to tell time as our world was lit with perpetual orange dusk from the fire, it was impossible to determine if we ate the regular three meals a day, or more. Or less.

We routinely pulled out the mini-scopes to peer through the glass down at what had been Terra. As we climbed ever higher, we were able to see farther and farther with the help of the portable telescope. But I almost wished I hadn't packed them. Each time, our eyes were greeted with the familiar wall of flame, blotting out any signs of life below.

We lay together each night, twining our bodies and softly speaking our love for one another. Some days ago, the black rocks had ceased falling.

Eventually, we reached the cloud cover. Luckily, our worksuits worked the same on the cold as they did on the heat. We moved ever upwards, traveling closer together so as to never lose sight of the one we loved. The only one we knew was left in the world. At least the ground was now hidden from our view.

One sleeping cycle, we lay together, looking into the other's eyes, and Rian said, "What do you think we will find?"

I gazed at her, falling into her beauty, even disheveled and smudged as she was from our journey. Her hair hung lankly about her head, and her face was so dirty that I could no longer see her pale-green glow. But she was my Rian, and she was with me. As long as we were together, we could survive anything. Even this. "I am not sure."

"Do you believe the Loctari have found us again? That this is punishment for our rebellion?"

"It has crossed my mind," I replied. "We've been free for years, but perhaps that is just how long it took for them to reach us."

Her eyes were sharp with thought; I could almost

see the mind behind them whirling away. Her grief had faded to the background days ago, and now her fierceness shone through. "I wonder what this is, then, if the Loctari found us," she mused as she patted the rock beneath us.

"Some sort of weapon, meant to destroy our world. Slowly."

"Yes, but what exactly *is* it?" she continued.

"Some sort of rock," I shrugged. "It doesn't really matter what it is, all that matters is that it's stopped targeting us. I want to believe that means the lunar colonies were successful in ending the attack."

Rian snuggled closer to me. "I hope you're right. And I hope they'll see the flares we send when we finally reach the top."

I rested my face against Rian's neck and willed myself to sleep. Despite my heart condition, the colonies would have to take us in as refugees. Our climb alone would have to be enough to convince them that I could survive the harsh conditions of either moon.

The next waking cycle, we had to don the life support helmets I'd packed a lifetime ago as the atmosphere began to thin too much to breathe on our own, even with our heightened abilities from the meal bars. We had seven days' worth of life support each.

A few sleep-wake cycles later, we crested the cloud cover. We stumbled forward a few more steps, and then sunk to our knees, clutching each other.

All around us, the dark gray clouds made up an artificial ground. Black rocks jutted upwards from the cloud-ground, appearing as dark dolphins slicing through the waves. There were hundreds of the fin-like shards that we could see, even without the aid of the mini-scopes. But what had dropped us was the view above.

Though we'd never before seen the space around our Terra in the flesh, we knew it was lacking. A darkness where one of our moons should have been. And a ship hovering above our other. The atmosphere of Luriel, the moon that still occupied its rightful place beside Terra was lit with blasts of fire spiderwebbing its surface, somehow caused by the ship in its orbit.

As the silent lights raged above our heads and washed our black rock with color, we took no heed. Instead, we turned to one another, allowing the other to become our entire galaxy. Rian's face filled my entire field of vision, her beauty spilled into my heart, and her love overflowed into my body. Slowly, we removed our gloves simultaneously, and allowed bare skin to meld together, so we could be whole.

"You are my only," I whispered to her, my voice carrying all of my hopes, the dreams we shared, my bursting, everlasting love for her.

"As you are mine," she replied, her amber eyes afire and her dirty, tattered skin burning a deep green.

Neither of us looked away from our love as our second moon was destroyed by the Loctari ship, and the shards of its demise hurtled toward Terra like so many dark dolphins.

About Nikki Mitchell

Nikki Mitchell is a writer, editor, and high school English teacher who happily spends her life traipsing through fantasy worlds. She began writing at the early age of five, but it was not until she discovered *The Wheel of Time* series by Robert Jordan that she truly found her passion in words. She was first published in *Beneath the Twin Suns: An Anthology* in 2020, and then again when she edited and published *The New Normal: A Zombie Anthology* in 2021. When not writing or lesson planning, Nikki is busy bookstagramming, hiking with her two German Shepherds, or playing D&D and board games.

Find out more about Nikki Mitchell below.

Website: thebookdragondotblog.wordpress.com
Twitter: @TheBookDrag0n
Instagram: @TheBookDrag0n

O, swear not by the moon
by J.L. Peridot

CHAPTER ONE

Asubroutine pours a drink for Roxy. Tanith studies the particle trajectories as fluid swirls inside the glass. So realistic—the latest patch to the Garden has all but eliminated the uncanny valley that reminds her she belongs to a different world.

"Do you want one?" Roxy gestures too wildly and splashes wine onto Tanith's lap. The stain blossoms perfectly with every millisecond. Its algorithm is magnificent. "I'm sorry, I'm not used to the new physics."

Tanith smiles at her cousin. "Don't worry about it. I don't feel a thing."

"Oh, really? Hmm, maybe they'll release the haptics

in the next update. Still impressive, though."

The subroutine chirps. *Cleaning will be forty credits.*

Tanith smirks. "But of course the developers completed *this* feature."

"I'll pay. It's my fault."

"Don't worry about it. It matches my hair tonight."

"*No*, this is happening. We can't have you looking shabby with *you-know-who* over there."

The subroutine rolls away and Tanith looks to the entrance of the virtual playground. *He* has arrived.

He calls himself "Faruk." Tonight, he wears green eyes and well-groomed eyebrows with a pair of slits cut into the outer crest on the left side. And last week, when he kissed her, Tanith could have sworn the Garden haptics had already been released.

"Try not to seem so eager," Roxy chides.

"But I *am* eager."

"Watch him in the corner of your eye, then. *Private on.*" She turns Tanith's face towards her. "Pretend we're talking about him. How was the flight to Sisal?"

"We shared a deck with the delegation from Remus. Mum made me keep my door open so she could make sure I was a) studying, and b) not 'having the boys over.' As if I'd do a thing like that."

"Reman boys are hot, Teresa, especially in their diplomatic class. Bred for positive relations, indeed."

"I can't even have *you* over, Rach, let alone some guy."

"You wouldn't anyway. You're a good girl, not like

'bloody cousin Rachel.' How are Auntie Brenda and Uncle Walter?"

"Same as always. They still don't know I talk to you. I think they'd cut off my access if they did."

"So never tell them, hmm? Your folks are the definition of 'Mangrove diplomat,' and I love them, but well, you know... Oh, here comes your boy. *Private off.*" Roxy postures with a sideways glance. "Faruk."

"Roxana."

"To what do we owe the pleasure?"

"To be in the Garden is itself a pleasure, no? My presence is then but a common thing."

"Blah-blah, I can't tell if you're being humble or an ass. Are you here to steal Tanith from me?"

"If she'll let me."

Faruk private-messages Tanith a memory of last week. It's a song of sighs and lips and skin and tongue; a memory so real and vivid, she shivers in her cosy room in Sisal City's Mangrovian Embassy. Her neura-link with the Garden flickers, only for a nanosecond but she perceives it fully. It's in the tiniest delay between smiling and sensing the feedback from her avatar.

She thinks to blame the connection, perhaps a solar flare interfering with the wi-fi, or her old hardware due for an upgrade. But in all honesty, the highest-probability reason is that she likes Faruk. *Really* likes him.

Roxy kisses her cousin's cheek. "I should get to work anyway. Fly away, lovebirds. Shoo!"

Jonas Meyer, the only son of Ambassador Meyer and her pink-nosed husband, tugs at his Mandarin collar. He looks as ill-fitting as Tanith feels, yet aesthetically a better match for the spartan decor in the Alpinian Embassy dining room.

He leans towards her. "So, what do you enjoy for your hobbies, Teresa?"

"I read."

"What do you read?"

"Books when I must, graphic novels when it's up to me."

"Ah, comics. I used to read those as well, but I outgrew them in highschool."

"And what do you read now, Jonas?" Tanith steels herself with a well-rehearsed smile, spearing the last crumb on her plate. If only the Alpinians would hurry up with dessert so she can go back to the Garden and chat with Faruk.

"Well!" Jonas's blue eyes sparkle. "For many years, I was *obsessed* with architecture to the point of completing a Masters in it. But in researching my thesis, I visited the Grand Archive on Planet Libros to study the rock walls in the basement levels and found I had quite the passion for history too. You see, their design suggests there may be man-made structures beneath the library that pre-date the founding of the city. Perhaps even the discovery of the planet itself. Did you know that, Teresa?"

"No, I d—"

"Neither did I! Well, it was both fascinating and irritating. History eclipsed my interest in architecture almost *overnight*. Can you imagine finishing a Master's thesis on a subject you no longer care for? But I must say, I very much look forward to returning to Libros. It's most pleasing that the Federation held firm on holding the summit there."

"Well, the summit *does* concern the people of Libros—"

"Then the people of Libros should be grateful to the Federation and cease their rebellious nonsense. In any case, perhaps once we're there, I might show you the Grand Archive?"

"Ah, did you hear that, Mr Meyer?" Madam Lee's voice trills through the room. "Our sullen offspring are becoming friends."

Tanith pretends not to notice her mother. "History's not really my first passion."

"Then what is?"

"Teresa's background is technology," Madam Lee interjects with pride.

Ambassador Meyer beams. "More concerned with the future than the past. Clever girl, Alpinia could use more like you."

"Is that remark aimed at me, mother?" Jonas sniffs.

"No, son, we all have our place and purpose in

society."

"I'll drink to that." Ambassador Lee raises his glass.

Concealed behind a hearty gulp, Tanith rolls her eyes at her father, almost spilling wine when her mother's hand lands on her arm.

"Our Teresa does work for that big social network, what's it called, darling?"

"The Garden, but it's not really a social network."

"Is that right?" Ambassador Meyer's smile fades. "And what kind of work do you do for them?"

"I don't work *for* them. It's just a hobby. Anyone can upload custom code to the Garden as long as it's within the guidelines."

"Mm, it's the 'anyone' part we find concerning. And the 'guidelines.' I mean, how much do we *really* know about the corporation running that 'platform'?"

"Here we go again." Mr Meyer chuckles. "We hear no end to this back home. And no points for guessing which side my better half is on."

"I don't approve of how entertaining you find me, Harald."

Jonas leans over again with a knowing grin. "In case you couldn't tell, our people are truly divided. But I think sanity shall prevail. That firewall won't be coming down anytime soon."

"Firewall?" Tanith frowns. "You... block access to the Garden?"

"Indeed, as part of our comms regulation protocol, essential for planetary security. The technology is *quite* impressive. You may wish to study it someday."

"I don't understand. The Garden is harmless."

"That's what they want everyone to believe, Teresa dear." Ambassador Meyer shakes her head. "But the corporation behind it is really no different to a planetary government in terms of power and influence. Hence, they should be sworn to the same Federation pledges and laws as we are. Alpinia boycotts them in protest *and* for the safety of our citizens. And I say the rest of the Federation should do the same. What say you, Walter, Brenda?"

Ambassador Lee clears his throat. "Now that you mention it, access to the Garden does represent a significant portion of Mangrove's interstellar network access."

"You see? That means influence! Not to mention the Garden can only strengthen anti-Federation insurgency movements, like what we've been seeing on Libros. Alpinian society benefits *immensely* from interplanetary relations through the Federation, and so does Mangrove. We could all do without such traitorous inclinations." Ambassador Meyer side-eyes her husband before baring her palms to Tanith's father. "You know, I'd like to learn more about Mangrove's external communications policies. So long as this doesn't constitute a betrayal of planetary state secrets."

Ambassador Lee beams. "Of course not. After all, our governments have mandated stronger relations. We've prepared statistics for the summit. I'll have my PA, Landry, send you a few reports. Most were prepared by our Teresa. She's a most competent officer under our cultural attaché."

"A woman of many talents, then." Ambassador Meyer raises her glass. "How about a toast—to sharing, to stronger relations. And, of course, to the Federation."

The Alpinian ambassador winks at Tanith, but it's a wink too sly and crocodilian. Tanith offers only politeness in return, relieved when someone finally arrives to clear her plate.

"You're being dramatic." Faruk teases her as they roll on a grassy hill in their private place. Tonight, he wears his hair in long tiny braids, and eyes grey with pinpricks that catch the golden light of a setting sun. His aesthetic makes it easy to forget about that unnerving dinner. "There are worse planetary capitals than Sisal City."

Tanith scrunches her face. The tedium of the last few weeks would have killed her by now if not for the Garden. In here, she doesn't have to be Teresa Lee, the only child of Planet Mangrove's Foreign Office—she's free to just be Tanith and spend time with Faruk.

"No, it's terrible." She nods. "I confirm it."

"So, you haven't seen the Mercantile Quarter? It's full of life, best district in that sector. Why don't you ask for a day off and go?"

"I'm not that desperate. My boss doesn't just *say*

no, he'll say it with a forty-five minute lecture that ends when his PA comes in to check his blood pressure."

"That... doesn't sound professional."

"Perks of working for your dad."

"Ah, a family business. I relate; it's an interesting beast."

"Doesn't matter anyway. We're leaving tomorrow." Tanith catches a braid and sticks the beaded end in her mouth, brushing the prickly tips of hair across her tongue. The realism is phenomenal.

Faruk grins. "You're doing that thing again."

"I'm just so impressed with these new haptics. Did you hear the next patch will be for smells?"

He replies with a kiss, sweet and sexy and inviting, and a thousand flowers blossom in that private place. He pulls away and catches the bead in his mouth with a suggestive smile.

Tanith runs a finger along his cheek. "Kiss me again."

"I could do more than just kiss you."

"I'm sure you could."

"But..."

"But?"

"But... I'd like to get to know you better first..." Faruk cringes at himself. "I'm sorry, was that too forward? I've put you off."

"No, not at all, I just..." She smooths her skirt — hyperreal texture to match this moment. "Do you mean that? Cos I'd like it very much. I want to get to know you too."

"I mean it. How about one for one? I ask you, you ask me."

"Really? Are we turning this into a game?"

"Is that your first question?"

"*No*! Fine, I'll play. Come, help me think of something to ask."

Tanith kisses him again. His lips are soft like real lips, warm and tactile. It's a kiss with tongue and another nanosecond's lapse in signal, all the light and chemistry of an entire universe compressed into a moment under a dimming sky. She melts into him.

He pinches her cheek. "Tans, I don't think this is helping at all."

"It did, I promise... I have a question, but it might be too soon to ask."

"You can ask."

"It's against the Garden rules."

"This is a private place," he assures her. "We make our own rules."

"Yeah, but... you could still report me. I'd lose my access."

"I wouldn't. Just ask. I won't answer if I don't want to."

"Okay..." She curls a braid around her finger. "What's your real name?"

"Ah..." He flickers and disappears.

Tanith scrambles to her feet, checks the pink-hued landscape and finds nothing. But she still senses his neuralink, so he can't have logged out.

"Faruk?" No answer. "Faruk!"

"Sorry, I'm here!" He reappears behind her.

"Was that too personal? You can just tell me. We don't have to do names."

"It wasn't. That was terrible timing and I'm so sorry. I have to go in a couple minutes. I thought I had more time, but something urgent has come up. I swear it wasn't you."

"Oh, thank God. I thought you were going to tell me to get lost."

"I would never!" Faruk pulls her in. "And I would love to do names with you. Should we maybe wait until we can talk for longer? This feels… intimate. It'll be rude if I just leave after. I won't be able to come on again for a few days."

"I don't mind if you don't mind," she assures him. "Honestly, I'm dying to know."

"You know what?" He tips her chin. "Me too."

They fast-forward to a night sky and kiss again. This time it's chaste, but they hold each other like a few days apart mean forever. The remarkable haptics make her feel like she's falling into him—or maybe it's not the haptics at all.

He touches his forehead to hers and sighs. "My name is Shafiq."

"Pleased to meet you, Shafiq." Tanith smiles. "I'm Teresa."

CHAPTER TWO

"Come in."

Madam Lee's personal cabin aboard the starship *Nepenthes* is one-and-a-half degrees too warm. In fact, everywhere aboard the high-security vessel is too warm, and the lack of external network access has not ceased in making Tanith's blood boil.

"Good, you're here, Teresa darling. Come see what I chose for you tonight."

"You didn't have to, Mum."

"Hah, who would do it then? *You*?"

"I can choose my own clothes."

"This summit isn't some throwaway visit to the outer colonies. If things go well, we could see big changes for the Federation *and* for Mangrove's position in it."

"I thought this summit was about making things better for Planet Libros."

"No cheek please, Teresa. You know exactly what I mean. Our planet has made great strides in interplanetary politics, but we have a long way to go. Now, every good impression starts with —"

"With the welcome dinner, I know."

"With how you present *yourself*." Madam Lee retrieves an outfit on a hanger, still sealed in its plastic garment bag. "*You* in particular need to be careful tomorrow, after that mess at the farewell luncheon back on Sisal."

"That wasn't my fault, Mum."

"Never mind whose fault it was. I told you not to get distracted by the Reman boys —"

"I wasn't even talking to them!"

" — but you didn't listen and now every news outlet on the network has a picture of your ruined Veyrat summer original. It looks like you threw up on yourself. You should know by now to order only white wine when you wear light colours."

"Mum, enough already, *please*." Tanith sighs and sits on an uncomfortable sofa. "Fine, I'll wear whatever you picked."

"That's more like it, my darling." Madam Lee smiles sweetly and unzips the bag. "Stand up, let's try it on."

The outfit is a knee-length cocktail dress made from crinkled pearlescent fabric, paired with a cropped blazer that hugs Tanith's body in all the wrong places. She has her father's shoulders, but her mother insists the dress and jacket fit just fine.

"Aiyah, it's only for a few hours. You'll get used to it." Madam Lee adjusts her daughter's tiny gold cross pendant so the clasp of the chain is perfectly centered behind the neck. She brushes down the sleeves. "There you go. Yellow, black, and white—you look very patriotic. We are *proud* Mangrovians and want everyone to know. Make sure you wear red lipstick, okay? We'll call a manicurist when we're close to orbit."

Tanith regards her nails and thinks about the arrival, all the network access she could want, and the mysterious gift Faruk left her in the Garden. It's enough to put a smile on her face.

"Sure thing, Mum. Whatever you say."

On Libros, the welcome event is a cacophony of crowds and colours, all crammed into a banquet hall that barely holds the capacity. Waitstaff bounce between tables of delegates, desperate to restore order.

"We are so very sorry, Ambassador Lee, Madam Lee." The pale-faced host bows his head again, glancing nervously at the Mangrovian party behind him. "This is—"

"Highly irregular?" Ambassador Lee suggests.

"Unprecedented, I assure you."

"I'm sure it is," Madam Lee mutters under her breath, but not before checking that no one would hear it but her daughter. "Make sure you stay in sight of our security, Risa. Even if you need the bathroom."

"The venue was a last-minute change, Ambassador, but we should have everything set up soon. Our government prioritises the safety of every off-world visitor. If you wish, I could—"

"Say no more. You're at liberty to leave us and attend to other delegates." Ambassador Lee is tolerant, but clearly bored. The grateful host skulks away.

"I bet they changed the venue because of last week's protests." Madam Lee tuts, laying her napkin across her lap. "This is what happens when you leave the rabble to their business—utter chaos. I wish the organisers moved the summit somewhere else."

"And what message would that send, Bren?" Tanith's father mumbles. "This chaos is precisely what we're here to fix."

"It's a lost cause, if you ask me. Libros was never interested in joining the Federation to begin with. They're a culture too interested in itself."

"And yet they're the custodians of all the culture in the Federation. Their libraries preserve histories other worlds have forgotten. Have some faith, my dear. They want this as much as the Federation does."

"A minority, maybe. Most would never accept a solution from off-worlders."

"Well, on that I agree, but we'll see what happens."

A waiter approaches with drinks. There's a pinch on Tanith's arm.

"Ow! Mum, what?"

"White wine only, Teresa. I will order for you."

The Mangrovians toast to the Ambassador's health and to the Federation. Tanith's parents are delighted to be so close to the delegates from Planet Alpinia. They talk at every opportunity between each course and speech.

Once the last dish is cleared away, Tanith nods to her father's stoic PA before slipping out the foyer to watch delegates leave. She sighs into her wine, staring through the big window overlooking the venue compound.

"Would that be a sigh of disappointment or relief?" comes a voice.

A tall man joins her by the window. He wears a tailored galabeya made from purple material Tanith doesn't recognise. It shimmers in the light and from certain angles, she's certain it shimmers in shadow too. There's a dignity about his posture and only the slightest accent in the way he speaks the Federation tongue. On cue, her weary game face is back on.

"Apologies," he offers. "I was just making conversation. We don't have to talk if you came out for the quiet."

"Sounds like you'd also appreciate the quiet."

He smiles. "If I can be honest, these dinners aren't my style. But we do what we must for the Federation."

"For the Federation." Tanith raises her glass.

"I see we have the same taste in overwear colours." He holds up a light-coloured garment draped over his arm.

"Yours looks more comfortable. Why aren't you

wearing it? It's freezing in here."

"Red beverages and light fabrics don't mix. Don't want my parents to think I've been shot. Wouldn't that upset the apple cart?"

Tanith laughs. It's un-elegant, but how novel to hear such an archaic choice of words! In spite of herself, she's warming to him—beyond her diplomatic facade.

"So which party do you belong to?" she asks.

"Maraj."

"Oh, interesting, your star system's not far from ours. I'm from Mangrove."

"Yes, I could tell by your flag-themed ensemble. Is this the fashion where you're from?" He is handsome when he smiles.

"Ha-ha—are you trying to offend me, Mr Maraj?"

"Why do I sense it would take a lot to offend you, Ms Mangrove?"

"Perhaps because you don't know me very well."

"That's fair, I don't. But you did seem familiar. It's why I came over. It would have been bad manners if we'd met before and I didn't say hello."

"And do I still seem familiar?"

"Yes, although—"

Tanith's terminal chimes. She knows what it means, and it stirs a mix of disappointment and relief. She dismisses the alert with a flick of her wrist.

"Excuse me. It seems the delegation from my homeworld is ready to leave." She leaves her glass on the windowsill and smiles again—this time, it's for real.

"Thank you for the conversation."

"The pleasure was mine."

There's something in the way he bids her farewell — the look in his gentle black eyes, perhaps, or the tone of his voice as he enunciates each word in their common language. It irks her as she crosses the tightly woven carpet, and it's only when her party bustles past that she realises who he is. She drops her handbag and turns.

"Shafiq?"

But he's already gone.

CHAPTER THREE

Sure enough, there's a Shafiq al-Habib named among the delegation from Maraj. Like her, he's an attaché-in-waiting but a fashion designer by qualification, with a reputation for being the worst polo player in the Marajan diplomatic class. It is some achievement.

"And I contribute code to this place," he adds, tossing a ball decorated with the topology of her home-world. It materialises from nothing and spins on his finger. "Do I captivate you sufficiently?"

"The axis is off by three degrees." Tanith swats the ball away. It disappears in a puff of gold feathers. There's a sparkle in his eyes — they chroma-shift and she adores it.

"Impressive particle dynamics, little one. But the Garden doesn't allow contributed code that interferes with other players."

"There's a non-interfering version out there. Just thought you'd like to see the original in here. Where we make our own rules."

He leans in close, 'til he's only an inch from her face.

"But you interfered with me, Ms. Teresa Lee from Mangrove. Aren't you afraid I'll report you?"

"So, report me, Shafiq al-Habib."

"Perhaps I shall—later."

His lips meet hers in a deep kiss. Their private place turns from spring to summer. Tanith laughs into him. He has her attention completely here and now in the Garden, as if she weren't alone in her room in the Libros City Embassy District. She delights in his fingers through her hair. The haptics—*ah*, but these are the only haptics that matter. And she is breathless when they finally break apart.

"I must see you again," he says. It seems more a confession than a statement. "In person."

"I'd like that too."

"How about tomorrow, if you can get the time off? Would you need to ask the boss?"

Tanith bites her lip. "I might just sneak out. As long as I'm back before lunch, I can still make my deadline. They won't notice. After the *Nepenthes* flight, I regret not getting out more on Sisal."

"Was it my gift that changed your mind?"

"Maybe. It was a nice touch, sending me a market-place scene. I loved the colours and lights. Was it a puzzle for me to solve?"

"A… puzzle?"

"Well, there were things like fish and spices every-where, but all I could smell were pineapple, mango, banana and lychee."

"Ah, the olfactory data. I didn't even think!" Faruk slaps his forehead. "You must have a very old model Neura. The new ones generate more complex smell perceptions. Let me arrange something. It's such a different experience. You'll love it, I promise."

Above them, the vanilla sky pulses as a toy piano plays the first few bars of a lullaby. Faruk sighs and rests his forehead on her shoulder.

"I should turn in."

"You have a bedtime alarm? Does it sing you to sleep as well?"

"Maybe you can sing me to sleep sometime," he teases.

"Not a chance. I can't sing, but I can do this." With a peck on the cheek, she sends a coded message through his rendered skin and modelled splines, shooting at the speed of thought via his neuralink.

He shivers and somehow she knows he shivers outside the Garden too. She mouths the word in synch as his Neura synthesises it for him in his language.

Habibi — darling.

Next morning, Tanith meets him at a pâtisserie across the road from the Grand Archive. This part of town is a hive of activity already, the air heady with the smell of coffee and baked dough, aftershave and cigarettes and business, though both Librosi moons are still high in the sky.

Faruk's style impresses her outside the Garden too. Today, it's a tailored suit jacket over a t-shirt, and eyes his natural colour.

"Have you been here before?" she asks, squinting against the sunshine at the sound of horns in the distance — must be a traffic jam on the other side of the city walls. She picks at her pecorino danish, too excited to be hungry, and how can she not be?

"No, never, but I've always wanted to visit, ever since I was a kid." Faruk gestures up to the towering dome that caps the Grand Archive's central building. "Whole systems of culture and history are catalogued here. Who wouldn't want to visit?"

His enthusiasm is almost like Jonas Meyer's but better, more inviting, more interested in what she thinks.

Tanith bites her lip and can't bring herself to say she's never thought about it. That she's got her hands full with eighty-page reports about her own planet's culture, with the Mangrovian diplomatic class's culture, with her parents' culture looming over her shoulder, telling her what to wear to which official event and why. It doesn't matter anyway — his excitement has made her wonder.

The far-off car horns still blare as they stroll towards the main entrance. The foreboding double doors slide open as a car, with its lone horn blaring, speeds down the street. A light flashes in the corner of Tanith's eye.

No, *two* lights—speed camera. She spares a thought for the poor soul who'll pay the hefty fines this planet imposes on nonconformists.

Inside, Faruk takes her hand. The doors close behind them and they leave the noise and politics behind.

It's easy to lose oneself in the Grand Archive. The silence and space, high ceilings and shelves upon shelves of books and scrolls and tablets and data crystals... they devour time.

They devour sixty minutes before Tanith thinks to check her watch. And she only does so by accident, after catching her reflection while sucking a fresh cut on her knuckle. Someone ought to put a warning on pulp paper memorabilia.

Another hour goes by as they flit between rooms, enjoying what was called 'music' in the twenty-third century. Finally, Faruk gets stuck at the Tower of Hanoi puzzle in the antechamber outside the Antique Algorithms exhibit.

"You know, it would take someone five-hundred-and-eighty billion years to finish this," he muses, moving puzzle pieces with no perceivable lag. It's as if he plays through a neuralink instead of via gesture sensors around the simulacrum. "I wish at least we could have all day."

"Me too. As far as first dates go, I've never had better."

"High praise indeed."

"You'll be a hard act for the next guy to follow."

"Guess I'll have to outdo myself next time." He offers her his elbow. She curls a hand into it.

The pre-noon sun blazes high when they step outside. Tanith shields her eyes from the glare in clean windows and polished surfaces around the street. She'll have a headache later, but for now she's perfectly content walking with her shoulder pressed to Faruk's side.

They stop at a crosswalk one block away from the Embassy District. He brushes a lock of hair away from her face with the same gesture he used on the Tower of Hanoi, only more careful and deliberate.

She rises to her toes and meets him with a kiss, shutting her eyes against the daylight and another speed camera somewhere. Faruk replies, soft and shy on her mouth, hands cupping her face and making a private world between them, their own piece of paradise with fingers on skin, lips on lips, and all unspoken intentions rolling from tongue to tongue. The Garden, the haptics — they have nothing on this.

Parting is like agony, but it's time. Tanith begins the walk of dread back to her Embassy.

The halls are empty when she arrives, only security guards and one lone receptionist in the foyer. Hearing her shoes *clack-clack* unnerves her en route to the inner sanctum. She pauses just outside the lunchroom and eavesdrops on the TV news.

There's talk of an incident outside the city. Everyone must be watching the live coverage—a distraction as good as any. She slips past and heads upstairs.

As she reaches her room, her neuralink registers a call from Landry.

"Yes?" Tanith drones.

"You're answering now. Does this mean you're done with those slides?" Even with xyr usual administrative monotone, Landry sounds irate.

"Is that why you've called me twenty-five times?"

"It seems you haven't checked your voicemails either."

"Was my answerphone message not clear?" But Tanith had lied in her message. She wasn't busy working all morning, so she has no right to snap at her father's PA now. "Never mind, I'm sorry. I've got things on my mind."

"Respectfully, Miss Teresa, you may soon have more."

"What does that mean?"

Landry sighs. Xe never sighs, and xyr precisely cultivated administrator's voice never sounds this tense. Something's wrong.

"Your parents wish to speak with you in person."

"I'll see them at dinner tonight."

"You'll see them now."

"Excuse me?"

"Just get up here, Miss Teresa. Please?"

CHAPTER FOUR

Tanith pulls her father's door shut, shoulders tense as his footsteps storm close.

The door opens.

"Don't you slam the door on me, Teresa Lee. Your disrespect is getting out of hand."

Ambassador Lee's face is darker than usual, wild eyes laser-focused, finger pointed at his daughter like a weapon. How she hates to see her father like this.

"I've shown you no such thing," she mutters.

"You listen to me. You will *not* see that Marajan boy again. You will stay in this compound until after the summit. And the moment we depart, you and your mother will begin preparing for your marriage to Jonas Meyer. There will be no argument."

He slams the door. Tanith's heart pounds like fists against a wall.

"If it's any consolation, it's better that you're grounded." Landry's voice cuts through the silence. Xe clears xyr throat. Between a long curtain and a fake fireplace, xyr pants suit blends in with the bland decor that surrounds xem. "What I mean is it's far safer in this district. Especially after the incident today."

"Whatever, Landry. Thanks."

"Wait. I'll walk you."

"You don't even know where I'm going."

"I do—where you always go after a confrontation with your parents. But even if you go elsewhere, I shall walk with you."

"I'm fine on my own."

"No, you're not. Here, have one." Landry offers Tanith a candy éclair and they walk. "Miss Teresa, this situation occurred because you went out on your own. Even just *one* bodyguard could have kept watch for anything pointed at you, gun or *camera*. Then these photos of you and Shafiq al-Habib of Maraj wouldn't be circulating on the network. And your father would not be upset."

"He would've found something else to get upset about."

"Granted, though with reason. You are important to Mangrove's future in the Federation."

"Important? Is that a joke?"

"I do not joke, Miss Teresa."

"They treat me like I'm a *thing* they *own*. But I'm a person, Landry."

"You are a *privileged* person. So privileged you don't even see it."

"Is this why you wanted to walk, so you could call

me a spoiled brat? Have you got that filed away in some special folder?"

Landry twitches. "That is not what I meant."

"Sure sounded like it."

"You were born into the diplomatic class, which affords you privilege and responsibility. To enjoy this life means playing by those rules. You cannot have one without the other."

"I don't need to hear this from you, Lands."

"I suppose you don't."

Outside her room, Tanith accepts another éclair. She tucks the wrapper into her pocket, fingers instinctively closing over a souvenir token from the Grand Archive. She thumbs its embossed emblem and suspects her body will make a habit of this soon.

Landry sighs. "I did not mean for our conversation to go this way. I only wished to convey my regret for your circumstances, though my feelings on this do not count. However, you look happy in those photos. Perhaps the happiest I have ever seen you. And there is… something else."

"What else?"

"Regarding your arranged marriage to the Alpinian…"

"What about it?"

Tanith only now notices that Landry has been fidgeting over xyr own candy wrapper since they stopped. She's never seen xem fidget until now.

"Your mother once revealed she almost did not

marry your father. She…" The PA's left eyelid twitches. Xe takes a wheezing breath and presses a hand to xyr heart. "A moment, please, Miss Teresa."

"Landry, what's wrong with you?"

"Merely psychosomatica. Administrators are conditioned against speaking of such things. Perhaps it may pass."

Landry closes xyr eyes and unwraps another éclair. As xe bites xyr lips shut and sucks the sweet, Tanith realises one privilege her class has afforded her. It is a reality she cannot un-see.

Finally, Landry finds a full breath of air.

"I was helping your mother prepare items for storage. I came across a picture of her and a man who was not your father. By the datestamp, she would have been somewhat younger than you are now. She looked just like you did in those photos from today."

"I… I had no idea. Who was the guy?"

"She did not say. I was not meant to see the picture. She burned it in front of me."

"Damn…" Tanith slumps against her bedroom door. "So, she almost did what my cousin Rachel did. But she *did* marry my dad in the end."

"So their families could consolidate power." Landry presses xyr chest again. "Together, they attained the Foreign Office position and achieved much for Mangrove. This is the directive of your class, Miss Teresa. This is what you were born to do. But you do not need to hear this from me."

When Landry leaves, Tanith retreats to her room. The sight of xyr like that is worrisome, but all she can do is collect herself in silence.

At the foot of her bed, she finds a white paper bag with her name in fine lettering. Inside is an object no bigger than a deck of cards, gift-wrapped and tied with a modest ribbon in the colours of the Marajan flag.

"I've been grounded," Tanith laments.

"Me too." Faruk bumps her shoulder in regretful solidarity.

"It's ridiculous. We're too old for this."

"We are, unfortunately, still the appropriate age for this." He throws a pebble as far as he can off the hill. It lands in the river with a splash. "On the bright side, it's better than my mother thinking I was anywhere near that car bomb outside the city. Finding out I was *only* out in public with a Mangrovian the day after they negotiated my betrothal — that might have been what saved her from a heart attack."

"Now that you mention it, I wonder if that's why my dad was more unreasonable than usual. He must have been worried about me. I'm glad no one got hurt. Well, except the guy who messed up planting the bomb."

"Come on, seditious anti-Federationists need sympathy too."

Tanith smiles dourly. The sky is apricot and gorgeous, but a dark cloud hangs over them both.

"Did you know about your engagement to that girl from Earth IV?"

"No, my family planned it without me. They wouldn't have told me until tomorrow if not for those photos of us. Did you know about the guy from Alpinia?"

"I had no idea." Tanith shakes her head. "Should we have seen this coming, Faruk? Was it a mistake to meet — out there, in here…"

"No, don't think that way. I don't regret it."

"I don't either."

"And I don't regret kissing you, only that we were recognised and photographed." Faruk throws another stone. This one gets lost in the rendered tree foliage swaying in the breeze. A plump peach falls out, squeaking as it lands.

Tanith cracks a smile, forgetting for a blissful moment how miserable she is. "That's new."

"I coded it before you got on. Needed something to cheer myself up." He puts an arm around her. "At least we'll always have the Garden, right?"

But they won't, and she isn't ready to break the news. Sucking in a deep breath, she's thankful for the sensory input from the new Neura. The Garden is ten times more vivid now — colours in motion, textures hyperreal, sounds resonating in her limbics, and the smells, *oh* the smells! It's the summer sun, river humus, the blades of virtual grass that snap as if for real in her hands, releasing the scent of moisture and meadows and living things. All wonderful distractions she can blame, should Faruk wonder why she hasn't yet responded.

He strokes her hair with a cradling touch.

"Thank you for the hardware," she says softly. "It's such a gift, especially now."

"Would you like to try the marketplace again? Did you keep it?"

"Of course I kept it. Let's go."

She grabs his hand and summons the file. In milliseconds, their hillside is overtaken by a thriving scene of goods and stalls and foods, paved steps and decorated archways leading to anywhere or nowhere, protected on all sides by rustic walls, domed roofs and minarets peering over from the other side.

The heat and humidity are immediate, along with the fruit smells Tanith remembers from before. But laid over it are smoke and spices, cooked meat, fragrant oils and tepid water from a nearby canal. Then there are the bodily aromas of passersby, the sunbaked stones beneath them, clay and clarified butter, and also...

One scent in particular tickles a vague place where old sentiments linger. It smells of familiarity—not hers, but his.

"Faruk, is this from your homeworld?"

He squeezes her hand. There's a longing in it—distinct, even through the neuralink. "My parents were assigned to the outer provinces just after I was born.

This is where I grew up, generated from my memories and historical records."

"It's magnificent, Faruk. This is your home."

"Better than home. This place will always be here, and I can still be myself, be happy in it. Maraj is home to my body, but this place is home to my soul. Now let me show you my favourite coffee shop."

They sip sweet tea and eat baklava at a tiny table. Faruk tells stories about each subroutine who walks past, as if he knows each one intimately. And why wouldn't he — after all, doesn't Tanith know by heart the personality algorithm of every pet she programmed and uploaded to the Garden?

A vegetable stand collapses three stalls away. The seller scrambles to collect his wares.

"Strange." Faruk cranes his neck to see. "That's never happened before."

"You didn't code that?"

"It's possible, based on the physics modules. But I didn't create that specific event. How interesting, I wonder if it's because you're here. The system learns, you see."

Tanith wrinkles her nose. "Great, I'm a curse on your adaptive algorithms."

"Variety is the spice of life, habibti."

The market becomes a different creature after sunset prayersong — there's soul, there's fire. Faruk buys her oil from a perfume stand. She dabs a little on herself, on him, enjoying the heady sandalwood fragrance mingling with the night air. They get caught up in the culture of this place, sights and smells, murmurings and music under a star-addled sky with three moons. Faruk names each one for her with words rolling like verses from a favourite poem.

They sit in a corner padded with rugs and cushions propped against the wall. An old man plays an oud outside an arcade of food kiosks as customers file in. They are subroutines, each and every one of them, and yet they seem so real, so *right-here* thanks to the Neura and the craftsmanship in Faruk's code.

And when Faruk kisses her, it's no different to this morning—fingers and skin, lips and tongue—as if they're flesh to flesh once more, tangible and concrete at the intersection of two busy streets. In just a few days the summit will be over. The future holds nothing for them; she can't walk away from family and neither can he.

It will hurt so much to say goodbye.

A tear rolls down Tanith's cheek, but still, she can't bring herself to tell him about the Alpinian firewall. Even if she could tunnel through and access the Garden, what good would that do? They'd be married to other people, honourably, with diplomatic duties to fulfil. But he already knows this. It sharpens the sting.

Her mouth remembers the taste of Shafiq al-Habib, reinterpreting signals from the neuralink. It's a scent and flavour so familiar yet so different from the other times he kissed her, before they met in person, when he was only an idea conveyed through a data stream. And now everything about him has left its mark, charred and indelible, across her heart.

Humans run on adaptive algorithms too, and finding him has put a curse on hers.

"I want more than just the Garden, Faruk."

He hugs her tight. "So do I."

CHAPTER FIVE

It's only six-thirty in the world of obligations. The Neura's time manipulation is diabolically cruel when used in the penal system, but it's a boon for forbidden lovers yearning for longer nights and just a few more hours in each other's arms.

Tanith leaves briefly to answer a knock. She tucks the used ribbon and giftwrap under the bed and leans her full weight against her bedroom door.

"Teresa?" Madam Lee knocks again. "You ready?"

"I'm not coming, Mum."

For the first time ever, Madam Lee doesn't insist, giving only a brief goodbye and a suggestion of room service. Landry's revelation comes to mind — about her mother, about *that photo* with *some guy*.

"Do you need to go?" Faruk asks upon her return.

"No."

Something catches Tanith's eye — a faint glimmer at the other end of the food arcade.

"Did you just add that?" She points, squinting

against the dim light.

"Add what?"

"That—ugh. Come with me."

They arrive at a door just two-thirds the size of other doors in the market. It's devoid of a knob or handle, but bears the emblem of the Grand Archive. Tanith reaches for the token before remembering that her avatar in the marketplace doesn't have it.

"Well, that's interesting." Faruk touches the emblem's metallic surface. "This is supposed to be a bare wall. The system must have generated it."

"From today?"

"I don't have another explanation."

Tanith grimaces. "I'm sorry, am I messing up your memories?"

"Not at all. I used adaptive algorithms because I wanted this place to feel real. Which means only some things stay the way you remember—others change with you. But this... Doors just don't materialise out of nowhere, and yet this one did." He grins. "And, of course, we're going in."

"Of course."

They stand at the summit of a rock-like formation jutting into space, surrounded by a sea of cloud cover. A planet hovers too close with webs of light decorating its night-time hemisphere. A distant star illuminates the other side.

"Where are we?" Tanith asks.

"I've no idea." Faruk shuts the door on his marketplace, leaving them immersed in this new scene. "Could this be from your memory?"

"I've never seen this before. Looks like we're orbiting that planet, but it feels too close to be a moon."

He stomps the ground and peers over the edge of the formation. "I wonder what's down there."

"Well, wonder no more. Let's go look." She turns and leads the way to cloud level.

"Hey, Tans? Think fast!"

Faruk's hard body crashes into her, wrapping around and pulling her close as momentum sends them both tumbling, giggling like children through the clouds.

They burst through the bottom. Where Tanith expects to see sky or void, she finds data—*torrents* of data—whizzing past them as they fall. Hairless apes around a fire. A figure in a primitive spacesuit planting a flag on barren rock. A generation ship imploding as it prepares to leave a star system, remnants caught forever in a nearby planet's gravity well. What they just saw, perhaps—but there's no time to wonder. Something uncanny flashes past.

"Stop!"

Velocity cuts out. The data stream recedes, leaving just one scene playing out before them.

"What the fuck…" Faruk moves closer.

"It's us, Faruk."

The Faruk in the scene swipes his hand across air and sighs. It echoes in the space around them. *I wish we could have all day.*

Me too, comes Tanith's voice behind him. *As far as first dates go, I've never had better.*

"It's from this morning." Faruk—her real one—puts a hand on Tanith's shoulder. She cuddles his waist. "Looks like security footage, so I guess… we're in the Grand Archive databanks? The marketplace algorithms must have generated a tunneling protocol from the Garden."

"All by itself? What kind of code do you write that it could do this on its own? Are you a cyberterrorist?"

"Uh, this stuff only started happening since you got on, so if anything, *you're* the terrorist."

He pinches her cheek. She laughs and swats his hand away with a slap and a puff of gold feathers.

"Huh, I guess that worked." Tanith scratches her head. "We could have some fun with this."

A notification tugs at Tanith's mind—the staff have left a tray at her door. It's a sobering reminder of a world that chooses her meals and outfits; and decides who she can and can't spend time with. Meanwhile, Faruk summons a handful of data packets and sifts through them with fascination. His curiosity is endearing.

Tanith dismisses the notification. "Let's enjoy ourselves tonight, Faruk."

Together they plumb the depths of the Grand Archive. They soar through the founding of the Federation and the ending of interstellar conflicts as newly minted members sign treaty after treaty.

When that feels like homework, they go back to the first generation ship that entered this star system, then further to the first colony fleet that left Sol, then further still to a time in human history when a despot ruled Earth Prime. They draw gold-feathered dicks all over his administration, exquisitely punch-drunk on data.

When Tanith falls asleep, it's the best sleep of her life, curled up in Faruk's arms while the amniotic flow of ones and zeroes shields them from the world outside.

When she awakes, her hangover is the size of a nebula.

"That's what I get for not eating," she mumbles into her pillow, still connected to Faruk.

And for neurologically playing out three days without sleep in a single night. Thank God for coffee.

"You have coffee already? Ugh... Next time, let's go easy on the time dilation."

Agreed... So, this means I get a next time with you?

"I wish it could be all the time."

Maybe there's a parallel universe where we're normal people. Where the Federation doesn't exist, and we alone determine how we live our lives.

The idea of it stokes a pain in her chest. She pulls the pillow over her face and holds back the tear that threatens.

Tans, before you go…

"Yes?"

I hope it's not too soon to say this; please tell me if it is. But I think I love you. With more of my heart than is sensible given we've only just met.

And just like that, the pain becomes a little sweeter. He makes her happy and it hurts.

Have I scared you?

"No, not at all. But we haven't *only just* met. And, uh…" She shuts her eyes and smiles. "I think I love you too, Faruk."

CHAPTER SIX

That evening, Tanith fails twice to form the neuralink. She's frustrated, desperate for Faruk's company, and eaten by a sense of obligation — to tell him about the fire-wall, even if it spoils the time they have left.

When her neural oscillations finally synch, she finds Faruk has already been in the Grand Archive for two hours in real-time.

He meets her with a hug that's different from before. There's an urgency to it that traverses the connection and grips her throat. He no longer wears his fancy hair and outrageous eyes, but his own hair and eyes, his own face and body from the outside world.

"Faruk, we need to talk." She chokes as she speaks.

"We don't. It's okay."

"No, please. I have to tell you something."

"It's okay, Tans. I already know. There's something you should see."

Faruk summons a scene. It's Tanith with her family at the Alpinian Embassy on Planet Sisal.

"The Alpinians recorded us? Without our consent?"

"Not them. Someone—*something*—else." He pulls another scene. "Look at this."

Tanith recognises the building. "It's the Grand Archive."

"Now look at this."

Faruk rewinds. The modern library deconstructs, and the city erodes to its foundations. But it doesn't stop there. Soon the planet reverts to a time before it was named Libros. And where the library stood, a different structure emerges from the dirt, taking shape as a strange civilisation un-collapses. It's a metropolis, then a city, then a village, then a primitive edifice taken apart by blurred figures to reveal a light emanating from an abyss.

"What are we looking at, Faruk?"

"We're seeing footage going back to… to… Tans, those scenes from Earth Prime last night weren't artistic renders. They were the real thing. We *saw* the real thing. Now look at this. It's the earliest record I could find in the, uh, the databank."

With a wave of his hand, the scene disappears into darkness and silence, leaving only a timestamp barely in view with digits cycling, increasing in length. Tanith applies a translation filter. In Hanzi, Arabic, Bengali, Old Roman—every writing system she can think of— they are numbers counting up from nothing.

Then there's a noise, a faint patter like rain on distant canopy. The patter becomes pink noise, then white noise, then a pulse. Then light and colour.

Then, an assault.

Tanith covers her ears, but it's not her ears that hear it.

Faruk takes her hand. "Just wait."

She hears him perfectly through the chaos.

Finally, the scene settles into the serenity and dim light of pre-dawn. Coherent shapes form in the shadows. They are lumps on what feels like a rock floor.

"What are these, Faruk?"

"A primitive people. They're asleep now, but further along there's footage of them going about their daily lives. Tans, I don't think the market tunnelled from the Garden into in the Grand Archive databank, but some *other* data source. According to these recordings, there's ancient architecture under the city, from before the discovery of this planet. There were people living here. They pre-date all of us and this was their home before they destroyed themselves. But this *thing* we're in, this data collector… it remembers. And it remembers other things too."

"Things from Earth Prime?" she asks.

"And from Sisal."

Faruk summons the footage from the Alpinian Embassy. Jonas Meyer smiles at her.

But I think sanity will prevail. That firewall won't be coming down anytime soon.

"Tanith, I know they block and monitor access on Alpinia. And I understand why you couldn't tell me.

Just thinking we may never talk to each other again...
I knew I was kidding myself when I said we'd always
have the Garden. We'll be married to other people, after
all. I just thought... I don't know what I thought."

He closes the dinner scene. The primitive people
sleep on, but a small one rolls over and nudges Tanith's
leg. Her breath catches in her throat. It's all too much.

She's in Faruk's arms again, but no matter how
tight his grip or how fierce hers, her body won't stop
shaking. Not even when he tosses all the footage away
so they can sit in silence. Any moment now, she may
shake herself out of the neuralink.

But minutes pass and that moment doesn't come.
Still, Faruk holds her.

"I don't want to marry Jonas Meyer."

"I don't want to marry that girl from Earth IV."

"I don't want you to either."

Faruk has brought the marketplace to them,
summoned in some empty recess of the data collector.
They sit in the cushioned corner, listening to a small
woman play a guzheng, her lithe fingers making magic
over the strings. The Neura's time dilation is set to
maximum, hangover be damned. Tonight, they put off
tomorrow for as long as they can.

Tanith has also taken off her fancy hair and fancy

eyes. It seems silly to keep them on. There is a truth about this place that overshadows the fashions they put on in the Garden. Instead, she wears the oversized shirt she wears to bed in the world of obligations, recreated from her memory and the data already in this weird, ancient system.

She picks at the fringe of a rug. It comes apart indistinguishably from the real thing. Between the Garden's framework, Faruk's marketplace code, and whatever this mysterious machine is capable of, Tanith decides this is now the real world. Life *out there* is merely a cruel dream.

They agree to tell no one of their discovery, lest corporate rules and interplanetary schemes pollute its purity. If the data collector is conscious, sentient, there must be a reason why it hasn't made itself known.

"You know," he begins, with a sad smile, "when we met at the café, I was already wondering how I might introduce my family to yours. I never figured it out, but I knew I'd wear something slimming around the waist."

She loves how he can make her laugh, even in the midst of this.

"I'd never thought about it," she admits. "Even though this is how our class does things, I thought I'd still get to choose. I would have chosen you."

The woman on the guzheng takes a break. Her absence leaves a hole in the market air, even with all the chatter from tables of patrons. Across the way, the tunnel protocol door is gone. Firelights now glisten across a table display that took its place. It is filled with glass sculptures from Tanith's bedroom on Mangrove.

Faruk sits up. "Why don't we get married?"

"We'd be stopped before we left the compound."

"No, not out there. In here—just for us, away from everything and everyone."

"It wouldn't count out there..." And as far as their peoples were concerned, it would have never happened at all. Tanith reaches for his arm. "It could just be ours."

"Something private and special. And immortalised in this place, along with everything else that's happened in the universe."

"And no one would need to know. Faruk, I love it."

"You do?"

She nods, with so much enthusiasm she really might sever the neuralink.

He rises to his knees and takes her hands in his. "Okay then, Teresa Lee—"

"No."

"No?"

"Just Tanith. It's who I am."

He wears the smile of someone who understands, who is relieved and kindred. And Tanith is assured of what her answer will be.

Faruk begins again. He asks the all-important question in the presence of infinite beings and strange machines, of timeless times and eternal scenes. Tanith answers yes, and they embrace again while numbers count up and up.

There is no precedent for planning a wedding inside an ancient data collector. Out of respect, Tanith and Faruk choose a male maazoon and female priest for a combined ceremony. Out of piety, they set up tribute tables to their families and homeworlds, selecting each native flora and traditional food themselves.

But there'll be no giving away of the bride like property, just two equals walking hand-in-hand through the market's winding artery. And there's no need for a contract or tea ceremony or mahr and shabka, but — *oh*, what a festival the reception shall be!

The bridal veil is an elegant thing, a Shafiq al-Habib design, which Faruk handcrafted for a university assignment. In the outside world, the original was dotted with tiny stones harvested from a planet that rains diamonds. In here, each sparkle is the code of a star borrowed from the sky above Maraj and Mangrove on the nights he and Tanith were born.

She weeps when he tells her. He catches her tears on his finger and adds them to the veil.

"What colour would you prefer?" he asks, comparing his handiwork to that in a scene of his graduation show. He desires artistic perfection.

"The original is perfect. It's my favourite shade of purple."

"But your dress?"

"I can wear a purple dress." Tanith scrunches her nose and flicks through yet another catalogue of uninteresting wedding scenes. "Not sure about these styles, though. Do you have anything more traditional?"

"How about modern-traditional?" He summons another catalogue. "I find they have a more timeless quality about them."

"Warmer. Although maybe I'll go exploring, try a few on while I'm at it. Unless you want help here?" She eyes the gold lanterns strung up along the marketplace arches.

"No, I'm done for now. Apparently, it's morning already in the outside world. I might go have a shower and get some work done." Faruk kisses her forehead. "Meet you back here tonight?"

"Of course."

When he's gone, Tanith leaps into a nearby river and lets the current carry her into the annals of history. She floats unnoticed through the dress fittings of queens and peasants from every culture, but is most excited when she stumbles upon cousin Rachel's wedding. There are no Mangrovian wedding customs in sight and Rachel — Roxy — shines brighter than the sun.

At the end of the river, there's a small lake with a door at its centre. Ripples form on the mirrored surface around it. Tanith makes her way over.

But where she expects to find a changeroom, she steps out onto a carpeted floor that feels unnervingly familiar. Rows of suits and dresses line the walls of what looks like a walk-in wardrobe. She recognises the outfit her mother made her wear to the welcome dinner on Libros. It seems so long ago now.

Voices drift in from outside. It's an argument—a bad one. Landry and...

"Mum?"

Landry holds a photograph. Madam Lee grabs a lighter from her dresser drawer and sets a spark to the corner.

Tanith acts fast. A copy of the photo is in her hands before the flame catches. She shuts the wardrobe door and sprints across the lake while three moons light the way to shore. She doesn't stop until she's just outside the marketplace, back in the safety of its atmosphere.

"Print!" she commands, and rushes to the outside world.

Daylight pours in through her bedroom window. It stings her eyes, but she rubs them hastily and stumbles to her pocket printer. She scratches a warm patch of skin beneath the Neura sensors as shapes appear on the paper.

Her mother's face is undeniable in the picture, but the way she smiles really does look just like Tanith. A less familiar person would find them identical.

But it's *the guy* who stands out as he looks lovingly at the young Madam Lee, back when she still went by Miss Brenda Chen. Tanith's heart races as the details develop on his face. She sits on the edge of the desk, thumb sweeping over the image, not quite believing what she sees.

"Faruk?"

CHAPTER SEVEN

There's a knock at the door.

"Teresa, it's Mummy."

Tanith shoves the Neura in her dresser drawer, and photo in her pocket. "Come in, Mum."

Madam Lee raises her eyebrows. "Still in your pyjamas, darling?"

"I'm working from here today. Is that all you came to ask?"

"Don't be like that." Madam Lee sits on the unmade bed and pats the spot beside her. "Come sit, I want to talk to you."

Tanith sits, wary and resentful.

"You are upset about the engagement." Madam Lee rests a hand on her daughter's arm. "It's okay, I understand."

"Do you, Mum?"

"This is our way of life, Teresa. We live in such luxury and this is how we give back. Look at Landry, xe's free to marry whomever xe wants, but xe pays the price of the administrative class. This is what it means to be part of our society, darling. Take and give. You don't want to end up like Rachel, do you? Cut off from everyone she loves and exiled outside Federation space?"

"But what if she likes it there?" Tanith fights the urge to reveal the truth about her cousin. That Rachel is in love and free of suffocating customs. She's *happy*.

"There's nothing for her out there. She would have had it so good if she married that boy we chose for her. She can't even come back to visit now. Mangrove society won't forget she absconded from her duty. If you do the same, if this is about that boy from Maraj—"

"It's not, Mum," Tanith lies.

"Are you sure? I think you're telling fibs."

"I don't want to be moved around the Federation like a game piece."

"Now you're being dramatic, Teresa."

"Does it matter anyway? Even if there wasn't someone else, I don't *like* Jonas Meyer. He's arrogant and obnoxious. Would *you* want to be with someone like that?"

"Aiyah, a lot of people are like that when they're young. He has a lot to learn, and you can help him. You can learn together. You think your father and I were lucky enough to get along when we got married? We weren't. We had to work for it, and now look at us. You never know how things will turn out, darling. You must do your best no matter what. Even in a marriage to

Ambassador Meyer's peculiar son."

"*Mum—*" Tanith swallows. "I need to ask you something."

"Hmm?"

She pulls the photo from her pocket and hands it over.

Madam Lee's hand flies to her mouth. "Where did you get this?"

"It doesn't matter. Who is that guy?"

"Did Landry give this to you?"

"*No*, it wasn't Landry. And it doesn't matter. Mum, please. Who is he?"

Madam Lee's brows knit. At first, Tanith fears an angry outburst, just like the one she witnessed from the wardrobe. But tears form in Madam Lee's eyes. She reaches for a tissue and fans the air in front of her, as if she can wave it all away.

"Mum, please, can you tell me?" Tanith asks again, when her mum has caught her breath.

Madam Lee nods and blows her nose. She is out of excuses.

"His name is Usman. We met at university, before I knew your father. We were boyfriend and girlfriend for two years. It was the happiest time of my life, second only to when you were born. We thought it would be harmless just to date."

"But?"

"But we fell in love." Madam Lee takes her daughter's hand again. "Usman is the uncle of your boy from

Maraj. When I saw the pictures of you, my heart... It was like seeing my own future—the one that never happened."

"What did happen?"

"Usman proposed the day after our last exam. Unofficially, of course. We said we'd each go home and make proper arrangements for our families to meet. Economically, it made sense—we could have brokered a deal for better interplanetary trade. A friend happened to take this photo after I said yes."

She touches the grainy imprint of Usman's face.

"I got home and told your grandparents. They were so angry. That's when I learned they had already arranged a betrothal while I was away. They wanted to wait until after graduation to tell me. Usman and I spoke only once after that, to say goodbye. His parents engaged him to someone in a different sector. And I was married to your father within the month."

"You didn't even fight for each other?"

"That doesn't mean it didn't break my heart, Teresa. But this is our way. It was my duty, his duty. Walking away from duty means walking away from family, from home. I look back now, and I'm so happy I married your father. It means we got to have you."

She smiles and cups her daughter's cheek. Tanith eyes are teary too.

"You've grown into a fine woman, Teresa," Madam Lee continues. "Daddy and I are proud of you, and we love you so much. Marrying Jonas Meyer will strengthen our ties with Alpinia. You'll have status in our society *and* theirs. You'll have security and your children will too. And you can visit home any time you want. Mangrove will be in your debt and the Federation will be stronger for it. This is why we do this, darling. Maybe one day our people won't need to anymore. But for now, this is how we make sure you have a good and happy life."

Madam Lee clutches the photo to her chest when she gets up to leave. But she stops at the door and returns it to Tanith.

"On second thought," she requests," please destroy this for me, darling. It's better if the past stays in the past."

"I will, Mum."

Seconds later, there is another knock on Tanith's door. It's her mother again.

"Darling, I almost forgot. Dinner tonight is cancelled. There was another incident in the city this morning. It's getting worse out there. Libros Home Affairs has advised all parties to remain in the Embassy District. They can ensure our safety here."

"Are you ready, habibti?" Faruk whispers. It fills a silence never before heard in the market.

"Let's do this."

The crowd erupts. Music begins to play, led by the old man's oud and small woman's guzheng. Tanith has a hard time keeping the smile from her face. These precious moments with Faruk are more important than ever. Who knows if they'll be able to access the data collector again? Tanith's life may change completely after she is married to Jonas Meyer, maybe even after she leaves Libros.

Instead of pushing her fears away, she holds them close. They drive each step through the market, strengthening her resolve to savour every nanosecond of this event—her true wedding, the one belonging to her heart.

They reach their corner, now padded with every kind of flower Faruk could find in the data collector. The maazoon and priest await with a smile.

Tanith means every word of her vows, as if they come from flesh and blood and soul. Her ring, gold with feathers intricately carved into the metal, sits solid and heavy on her finger.

And when at long last Faruk kisses her, she finds he has stolen her trick! A coded message travels through her rendered skin and modelled splines, shooting at the speed of thought until finally her Neura synthesises it for her in her language.

Ai'ren—lover.

Their room is a rented suite above the market. Faruk never coded a hotel here, but the perfume seller arranged everything. The happy couple sit together by the window, sipping rose oolong cocktails by candle-light, watching dancers and artists entertain the crowd below.

Finally, they shut the curtains and undress. Tanith kept her promise to wear her actual shape and size, as honestly as she could make it.

It wasn't hard. Sometimes mirrors lie, but this ancient recorder collects only the truth. She copied her body from this evening, freshly showered, just before putting on her Neura.

Faruk is a sight to behold. He is so tall, firmer in some places and softer in others than she expects, but this is all of him as accurately as he can estimate, after factoring in food and drink and afterparty fatigue, and Tanith loves every bit of it.

Besides, he is firm enough where it counts on a wedding night, and that's all that matters now.

"I'm sorry we couldn't do this for real," she laments.

He tips her chin up. "This is real enough for me. Is it for you?"

"Absolutely."

CHAPTER EIGHT

Tanith jolts awake. Her room is dark, but light seeps in around the edges of her curtains. She touches her Neura—still firmly on. Something else must have woken her up.

She takes a swig of water and flops back onto her pillow, running her arms and legs across cool sections of bedsheet. When she fell asleep, it was beside her true husband, after a good and thorough wedding night. Her body gets warm just thinking about returning to him. But she needs the bathroom first.

She washes her face and studies herself in the mirror while she pats dry. On a whim, she smiles. It flows so easily from her eyes.

A call arrives just before she's back in bed. It's Landry.

"Good, you're awake."

"Why are you calling so late?"

"There have been attacks across the city. Home Affairs think this district is next. We're being evacuated.

You need to get dressed now."

"Excuse me, *what*?"

"This isn't a drill. Security's on the way—"

There's a knock at the door and a man's voice on the other side. "Miss Teresa!"

"Landry, my parents—"

"They'll be downstairs. Bring only essentials. There won't be room in the car for luggage."

"Miss Teresa?" comes the voice again.

"Coming!"

The lights come on. Tanith scrambles about the room, getting dressed, selecting only necessities and stuffing them into a backpack. She's alert and cognisant, heart rate a steady one-thirty from having rehearsed this process so often in safety training.

She is calm enough to peer through the neuralink into the bridal suite. Faruk is no longer there. She sends a ping. He answers immediately.

Tanith, are you okay?

"I'm fine. We're being evacuated."

Us too. It's chaos here.

"Miss Teresa, we must leave."

"Faruk, I have to go."

Me too. Stay safe.

"And you... Faruk?"

Yeah?

"I'm sure we'll be fine, but just in case... I love you. So much."

I love you too, habibti. With everything I am.

"Miss Teresa, *now!*"

Tanith throws open the door. Three guards rush her through the hallways, past vases and paintings bumped out of place, some already on the floor.

Her parents are waiting at the bottom of the stairs. They greet her like they'll never let her go, until more of their detail arrive to escort them away.

Outside, a blast of wind almost blows Ambassador Lee's hat away. Tanith catches it and pulls it firmly down on his head. A boom in the district rumbles the ground. The ambassador pulls his daughter close, squinting against the gale as a shuttle approaches the landing pad.

"Landry," he shouts over the engine and blades that cut the air, "you said we were taking a car."

Landry looks up from xyr terminal. "Change of plan, Ambassador. It's no longer safe for off-worlders here, especially ones representing the Federation. We're leaving Libros."

"Where's my chief of staff?"

"He was in the city, sir. In the first area that got hit. We haven't heard from him."

A fire illuminates the hill of the Alpinian Embassy. The blinking lights of a departing shuttle lift off from behind the building. There's another boom, another rumble — closer than the last.

Madam Lee kisses Tanith's head. "Don't be scared, darling. We'll be okay."

Tanith adjusts her jostled Neura and tightens the straps on her backpack. Across the district, shuttles ascend into the darkness. The starships waiting in orbit are indiscernible from stars.

A strange meteorite careens upward, rising from the tree line to the south. They see the explosion before they hear it.

"Oh my God…" Madam Lee grabs her daughter's arm. "They're shooting them down, Walter."

"Sir, Ma'am, we have to go."

Once inside and buckled in, Tanith thinks she hears the pilots discuss evasive manoeuvres, but it's hard to tell with the doors open and the engines still roaring outside.

What she does hear are the murmured prayers of her parents across the aisle. Somehow, they seem so loud, even with Landry just behind her, swearing as xe tries to reach the chief of staff again.

Out the window, another shuttle explodes in the sky.

The doors close and their captain announces the take-off protocol.

The lights go out.

"Faruk? Are you there? Please pick up."

Gravity pushes her into the seat as they lift off.

"Faruk, are you okay? Answer me, please…"

Tanith? Tanith, we –

"Faruk?"

The lights come on.

CHAPTER NINE

At first, there's only silence. Then comes rain on distant canopy. Tanith swears she's heard it before.

She brings a glass to her lips. Red liquid sways inside. It tastes like memory and truth.

She sets it on the windowsill as footsteps on carpet stop beside her.

"I knew you'd find me here," she says.

"Where else would you be?"

His hand is warm and welcoming. She thumbs the engravings on his wedding band.

The view from the window is breathtaking — a planet rising from a sea of cloud; a distant star illuminates its hidden hemisphere.

"Something has happened, Faruk. I don't know how I got here."

"Nor do I." He squeezes her hand. "What's the last thing you remember?"

"Our shuttle taking off, then nothing. What about you?"

"We were in a car, heading to a landing pad in another compound..." He fidgets. "Do you think we're dead?"

"I don't know. I don't feel dead... Do you?"

"No. I don't think so.

"I mean..." Tanith sips again. This time, she tastes wine. "We could have survived. Maybe you made it back to Maraj and married the girl from Earth IV. She's so graceful and you fell in love and forgot about me."

"And you returned to Mangrove. You married the Alpinian and had beautiful children."

"With *him*?"

"Any children you make would be beautiful."

"We could always check," she suggests. "The data's all here. We'd know for sure."

He smiles. "I know for sure it wouldn't make a difference to me."

"Me neither."

Faruk puts an arm around her. There is a wonderful realness about it.

About J.L. Peridot

J.L. Peridot writes love stories and more from her home beneath the southern skies. In her spare time, she nerds out over cryptic crosswords, calisthenics, and mechanical keyboards—all while dreaming of cyberpunk cityscapes and retrofuture romance.

Find out more about J.L. Peridot Below.

Website: jlperidot.com
Twitter: @jlperidot
Instagram: @jlperidot

The Arrangement
by Pamela James

"Rayan, where are you?" D'Iyla looked at the horizon. The sky was starting to brighten with the first of two suns fighting its way up. D'Iyla glanced back at the path, hoping Rayan was there. It wasn't like him to be late, and she was starting to worry that the prince's men finally caught up with him. "Khange khodah" she cursed. We shouldn't have separated, she thought. D'Iyla thought back through the past few weeks and how much her life had changed since meeting Rayan. That one day...

D'Iyla was late getting to the market and Nani, her

grandmother, wasn't going to be happy with her.

Pongal, the harvest festival just ended and like everyone else, D'Iyla was tired. They all worked extra getting all their fruits and vegetables harvested, working longer hours at the market selling all the produce, and now, preparing their food supplies for the cold season of Hinu.

"Navasi, hurry! The market is already open."

"Yes, Nani, sorry."

"Your wrap already has a stain on it. You need to be more presentable now that the prince has chosen you."

"I doubt he would like me working at all, grand-mother."

As D'Iyla put on her apron, she glanced up at the hill and the palace. It looked down over the village.

She had been up there only once a few months ago. She was amazed how far she could see from up there. D'Iyla had helped her father deliver the weekly supply of roti, the sweet green fruit her family had been growing for generations. Her family grew lots of fruits and vegetables but were known for their roti. It was then when Prince Imraan first saw D'Iyla and had contacted her father for a meeting. Her parents and grandmother were thrilled, Tata, her grandfather was hesitant like D'Iyla. Her parents had met with the royal family but D'Iyla wouldn't meet the prince until their wedding day. A union agreement was still in negotiations. It seemed like the rest of her life was now arranged.

D'Iyla didn't know much about the prince and life at the palace but of course heard stories from Boulo, her mother. "He is young and handsome! Praise to Ganesh he noticed you" her mother had told her.

"Your work soon will be as a wife and mother, but for now, put out the roti."

"Yes, Nani."

D'Iyla 's work went slow; it usually did when she was tired. There were less people in the market with the festival over, and fewer coming into the stall. About closing time, a small group of women walked in. They were well dressed and smelled of fresh flowers. Her mother had always told her these groups of women could be from the palace and to be extra courteous. These women didn't appear to be shopping for anything in particular, just looking around and gossiping.

"I heard the prince has found another consort."

"From where?"

"I heard he found himself a market girl."

D'Iyla's grandmother looked at her and put a finger to her lips. Their arrangement was to be a secret until her veil was removed at the ceremony.

"She will never fit in if she doesn't have any royal blood! What was he thinking?"

The women moved on to the next booth, tongues running as much as their feet.

Being so busy, D'Iyla hadn't given her new life much thought, and now she couldn't think of anything else.

"Don't pay attention to those women. They are just jealous they weren't picked. You will have servants to attend to you and all the parties! You will have a great life."

"Yes, Nani," she replied with less optimism.

Nani took the soar cart home but D'Iyla chose to walk. It wasn't far but she wanted some time alone as the house was rarely quiet.

The more she thought about it, the less she knew how life would be like. What she did know was that she would be a fish out of water.

She could hear everyone talking before she opened the door. They would be at the table, ready for their evening meal. As soon as she opened the door, the chatter stopped. It was obvious they were thinking about her life too.

"Come sit, D'Iyla," her mother pulled out the chair at her normal spot beside her. "We have been discussing your arrangement and we will be making the final barter soon. Your grandmother will move into a small cottage on the land behind the palace, but your grandfather wants to remain here on the farm. Part of the contract is that any of your family who cannot care for themselves, the Royal Family will care for. You know her health has been declining, plus she will be there to look over you."

D'Iyla just nodded, she didn't know what to say or if there was anything to be said.

The discussion continued but D'Iyla's mind and thoughts wandered. Her life was about to change drastically. She felt as though she was about to get on a spaceship without knowing the destination.

She slept uneasily. Her thoughts would not leave her brain and kept her awake for several hours past everyone else going to bed.

Her alarm woke her after what only felt like a few minutes of sleep. She rubbed her eyes, wondering if there was any way to get a little more sleep before she was summoned for her morning chores.

"D'Iyla? Are you awake?" Her mother slid her door open.

"Yes, Boulo", she sat up in bed.

Her mother crossed the room and sat on the bed beside her. "I am sorry".

"For what, Boulo?"

"We have been talking with everyone about the agreement, everyone but you. Are you ok?"

"I am not sure how to feel. I am a little excited, but I am scared."

"I know you are. I was too when I moved here after I was married. I didn't know how to be a wife."

"But you knew Baba and fell in love. Will I ever love the prince?"

"I am sure you will! We can talk more later tonight, ok?"

"Yes, Boulo."

It was still dark out when D'Iyla went to the barn. The sirin were clucking quietly as D'Iyla checked under each one, gathering the small pink eggs. They would be part of the family breakfast but D'Iyla wasn't hungry.

D'Iyla rode in the back of the soar cart with the produce while her mother and grandmother were up front. It hovered slightly above the ground. D'Iyla dangled her feet, and they hit bumps in the road. The morning air had a slight chill to it, and she pulled her feet up to cover her legs with her wrap.

The market opened as quietly as the day before, so her mother sent D'Iyla out with a short list of things needed for home. She walked slowly down the aisles. Even though she was at the market most days, it wasn't often she got to look at other booths.

D'Iyla stopped to look at new wraps. Hers was getting worn. It was silly to look as her mother would just make her another one or she would get a hand-me-down but she needed a distraction. Silly girl, she told herself. Soon she will probably have a closet full of new wraps.

After getting all the items on the list, D'Iyla stopped to adjust her now full bag. She glanced across the street to a small group of people. It was Prince Imraan. He was surrounded by a few escorts and guards and a few villagers trying to sell him their wares. D'Iyla stepped back into the shadows so she could watch her future husband.

The prince was very handsome, pale skin and short dark hair. His dark blue robe and pants were no doubt made of the finest silk. The villagers were vying for his attention, the guards were trying to keep them at bay. The prince just ignored all the noise. He seemed to walk through them like they were mist. A little boy ducked underneath all of the others and reached the prince. He looked as though he was selling a toy of some sort and got right next to the prince. He was dirty and wearing clothes a little better than rags. He looked to be about 10 years old and reminded D'Iyla of a younger cousin of hers. The boy reached up and tugged on the prince's robe at the same time the prince turned to head down the next row of booths. With the opposing movements, the pocket on the robe was torn half off. The boy quickly backed away as the prince stopped suddenly. Prince Imraan turned to look at the boy, his smiling carefree face contorted into anger. His arm flashed out, grabbing the boy's shirt. The prince drew him closer to talk. D'Iyla was too far away to hear the exchange of words, but the prince must have gotten his answer. He released the boy, but it must not have been what he wanted to hear as the next movement was the prince backhanding the boy. The boy was struck across the face with enough force to put him onto the ground. A quiet gasp escaped D'Iyla and she covered her mouth with her hand.

The stunned and now bleeding boy started to cry as the guards rushed over to him and hauled him to his feet.

D'Iyla was frozen in place. She was scared for the young boy and shocked with the prince's reaction.

A crowd started to form around the scene, but no one stepped forward to help the boy.

"Wait," a voice cried out from the crowd. "It was all a mistake, my brother did not mean any harm."

The statement came from a young man fighting his way to the boy. The man had long light brown hair that was pulled back in a tie.

D'Iyla could not see his face as he was facing away from her. The man was standing between the prince and the guards holding the boy and appeared to be calmly discussing the matter. He reached into his pocket and brought his hand out, extending it towards the prince without approaching him.

The prince finally noticed the growing crowd. He immediately turned his rage back into a smile, held up his hands and shook his head, refusing the rupees the young man was offering. The prince waved his hand, and the guards released the boy and started to disperse the crowd.

D'Iyla's attention was now drawn to the young man who knelt down to check on the boy. With gentle hands, he examined the boy for injuries. The young boy must have been ok as the young man stood up, took his hand, and led him away. They turned toward D'Iyla's direction and she was once again frozen, watching them walk closer. The young man was tall and muscular, his tunic hugging his arms and chest.

D'Iyla took a few steps out of the booth and shadows. As she did so, the young man noticed her, and their eyes met. Her dark brown ones to his emerald green. His calm demeanor seemed to ripple for a moment, he nodded to her and turned the corner away from where she stood.

A few minutes later, D'Iyla stepped back into the family stand, just in time. Shona from the next booth was already speaking to her mother and grandmother. It seemed that the event report travelled more quickly than she did.

"It all happened so fast," Shona said.

Gauri noticed her daughter. "I am sure the prince didn't mean to hurt anyone." She looked at D'Iyla and smiled.

Her grandmother ushered Shona back to her booth.

"Did you hear about it?" her mother asked.

"I saw it!" D"Ilya exclaimed.

"Are you ok?"

"I think so, it was just all a little unsettling, he seemed so angry."

"Maybe he was just having a bad morning. The prince must have many responsibilities".

"Yes, I am sure you are right," D'Iyla answered

quietly.

The rest of the day was uneventful which D'Iyla was grateful for. There was excitement at the table that evening. D'Iyla figured everyone wanted to talk about the occurrence in the market but didn't because of D'Iyla. Her grandfather seemed even more quiet than usual.

After helping clear the table and clean the kitchen after eating, D'Iyla headed out to the barn to check on the sirin and feed the other animals. She pushed the barn door open, and the light was already on, and her grandfather was in there, smoking his pipe.

"Tata, everything okay?"

"Yes, well, no, Navasi."

"What is wrong?"

"It's this arrangement, but I'm not supposed to talk about it."

"Why not?"

"I don't agree with it, and I worry about you."

She looked at her grandfather, not sure if she should talk about all her thoughts and feelings but he was always so easy to talk to.

"D'Iyla," he rarely used her name, usually called her Navasi, grand-daughter. "Tell me how you feel about all this."

D'Iyla broke down and ran into his open arms. "Tata, I am so afraid, especially after what I saw today. What kind of man is he?"

"I am not sure, Navasi. I have heard many

stories, both good and bad. He had all his charms out at our meeting and seemed very nice, but."

"But what Tata?"

"I guess I just wanted to hear your thoughts."

"I think I would have a good life, and he would care for you and the family. I don't see that I have any other choice."

"You always have a choice, Navasi. I may be an old man, but I can help in many ways, you need only to ask."

D'Iyla hugged him again.

"I made something for you."

She smiled. "What is it?"

He held up a thin leather band. "It's a bracelet."

"It is beautiful! It is just like yours". She held it near his thicker one he always wore. "What is this?" She pointed to the imprint on her bracelet. It was a circle with two crossed sabers with an ancient symbol below them and one above them.

"That is my mark of protection for you."

She slipped in on. "I love it! Thank you."

He waited quietly for her to finish her chores, and they walked back to the house.

The market was busier the next day and time flew with a steady stream of shoppers. D'Iyla's brothers Aadi and Deependu brought more produce near midday so they shut down the booth to eat together. Many other vendors did the same, it was a welcome break today.

People were still talking about the prince's incident yesterday. Even though D'Iyla saw it with her own eyes, she heard so many different accounts of it. As she was putting out more roti, her thoughts went back to all she saw yesterday, and she didn't notice the young man walk up to her.

"Sannu," he said quietly to her. She didn't hear him and kept up her work. He smiled, just content to watch her for another moment.

"D'Iyla," a voice broke her thoughts. D'Iyla turned her head towards her mother.

"You have a customer".

D'Iyla returned her attention to the table in front of her. Dear Kama, she thought, he is right here in front of me.

"Sannu," he said once more, a little louder.

"Sannu," she returned his greeting and bowed her head slightly.

Their eyes met but neither said another word. Collectively they were shy, excited, and nervous.

D'Iyla found her voice "Can I help you?"

"I, ah" he started to speak. He had been walking by and had seen her out of the corner of his eye. His legs had brought him to her before his head thought of something to say. "What do you recommend?"

Either her brain didn't send the words, or her

throat wouldn't let them out as she stood there for a moment, unable to speak. D'Iyla bit her lip, took a breath and her voice came out. "We are known for our roti. Would you like to try a slice?"

"Yes, I would," he replied, continuing to observe her every movement.

She grabbed a ripe roti in her left hand and removed the knife from the sheath on her hip with her other. She had been wielding a knife almost her whole life for many farm related chores and she handled it expertly. Within seconds, the roti was in slices and she offered him one.

He took a bite and closed his eyes so he could concentrate on the taste of the fruit. Now it was her turn to watch him. He smiled as he chewed. He swallowed and opened his eyes. "I can see why you're known for it. I think it's the best I have ever had."

"Thank you."

"Can I have four please?"

"Of course."

She picked out the best ones in front of her and put them in a bag. "Two rupees please."

He pulled out two coins from his pocket and held them out for her. Her fingers brushed his palm as she grabbed them. She gave the bag to him.

"I'm Rayan."

"I'm D'Iyla."

"If my family likes them, can I come back for more?"

Her face lit up with a smile. She nodded and whispered, "yes."

He touched his forehead, tipping his head as a farewell gesture, turned, and left.

D'Iyla watched him walk away and felt lighter than she had in days.

The conversation around the dinner table later turned back toward the arrangement but D'Iyla's thoughts were of Rayan. This mysterious man who surprised her again by appearing in front of her. She was trying to commit every detail of him to her memory. He was several inches taller than D'Iyla and his physique seemed even more defined up close. His green eyes were so bright. If they could see into her soul, she would let it happen in a heartbeat.

"D'Iyla!" Her mother commanded her attention. "The meeting will be in nine days."

"What meeting?"

"Haven't you been listening? The prince has changed protocol. You finally get to meet your prince," her mother stated, beaming at D'Iyla.

Her mother and grandmother went back to discussing it without her. D'Iyla was silent, her thoughts bouncing between Rayan and the prince, fantasy and reality. It took her awhile to fall asleep that night with all the activity in her brain.

The morning market was hectic, as busy as a hive of calponias, buzzing and alive. D'Iyla was grateful for the distraction, having to keep her mind on work and away from her life. Finally, midday break arrived. She grabbed her portion of the meal and headed towards the edge of the market where there was a park. She was searching for a quiet place to sit, to either sort through her thoughts or escape them.

She used to play in the park when she was younger and although she didn't visit it much anymore, it was still a special place for her. She walked to the far end of the park and found her favorite spot. A meadow that she could watch the Nellin river float by. The suns warmed her and all she could hear were the birds chirping and the water splashing on the rocks. D'Iyla took a deep breath and tried to release her stress with her exhale. The peacefulness of her surroundings was seeping into her.

"D'Iyla?" A male voice quietly entered her ears.

She turned and faced the voice. Rayan stood there in the sunshine, looking at her. "Am I intruding?"

"No, you aren't at all."

"May I sit?"

"Yes," she answered quickly, trying not to show her sudden nervousness.

"This is one of my favorite spots," Rayan said, gazing out onto the river.

"Mine too."

"The view, the sounds, and the smells. It's all

beautiful!" Rayan turned his gaze toward D'Iyla.

D'Iyla blushed. "And it's an even better place today. Did your family like the roti?"

"Oh yes, I've been sent back for more, that's why I was looking for you. I hope you don't mind me tracking you down here?"

"I don't mind at all," D'Iyla replied, unable to hold back a smile.

Small talk ensued. They talked about the festival, the market, and the weather.

"Well, I need to get back to work," D'Iyla sadly admitted.

"Do you eat here often?"

"Not as much as I'd like, but often."

"Will you tomorrow?"

"Perhaps." She smiled.

"May I join you?"

"Yes, I would like that very much," D'Iyla boldly said, looking up at him.

"I am already looking forward to it." Rayan stood up and extended a hand. D'Iyla took it and he helped her up. He bent over and surprised her with a sprig of trifollium. It was a small purple flower that had a sweet fragrance. "To remind you of me, until tomorrow," he said as he gave it to her.

She took it from him, took a deep sniff to add to the memory, and found herself smiling from ear to ear again.

They walked back to the market and said their

goodbyes, after he purchased more roti. D'Iyla tucked the flower into a buttonhole in the shirt under her wrap. She wanted it closer to her but also wanted to keep him a secret all to herself.

The next day, the midday meal could not come soon enough for D'Iyla. When it finally did, she had to stop herself from running to the park. When she was close, she saw he was already there, waiting for her.

"Sannu," she said to him as she sat down on the grass next to him.

"Sannu."

They talked, laughed, and ate while they sat in the warm sunlight. D'Iyla started asking questions, to learn more about him. Rayan lived with his family close to the middle of the village. He was a builder and loved building houses for families to live in.

He asked questions of her too. He learned D'Iyla has two older brothers, and her favorite fruit was now his as well, roti.

Her break time went too fast and they both needed to get back to work. Rayan helped her up again and again he picked her a fresh sprig of trifollium.

The next few days were similar to the last few with D'Iyla and Rayan meeting in the park, a fresh flower, and him walking her back to the market. She spent the rest of the time thinking of him and their next meeting.

The following morning as they were getting the booth ready to open, D'Iyla's mother came to her. "You have been working so hard, why don't you take the afternoon off?"

"Are you sure? It won't be too busy?"

"We can manage. I think it would be good for you to have a little free time."

"Thank you, Boulo."

At midday, D'Iyla continued with her new routine and went to the park to meet Rayan. Talking with him was getting easier but her butterflies were still fluttering in her stomach.

Between bites of her sandwich, she asked more questions about his work. He answered them all and had stories of the families that lived in the houses he built. "I could show you them some day."

"Do you have to go back to work today? My mother gave me the rest of the day off."

"I should go back for a little while but could show you some after if you would like?"

"I would enjoy that immensely!"

"Well, let's go then." As he helped her up, the wind blew at the tunic sleeve on his arm, exposing a tattoo.

"What is that?" she asked.

He bent over to grab a flower but instead of giving it to her, he turned and looked at her. She had taken time to braid her hair that morning and he wove the flower into her braid. He also tucked a stray piece of hair behind her ear and cupped her face with the same hand. He stared into her eyes and gently kissed her lips. "That's a secret," he said and winked at her. He stood straight up, lightly caressing her face. He grabbed her hand, and they started walking back towards the market.

The new house he was working on wasn't far from the market. Rayan found her a comfortable place to sit and quickly finished the task that needed his attention. With that done, the rest of the day was theirs. He took her from house to house, telling her of each uniqueness he put into them. He told her of minor details and specifications that D'Iyla found fascinating. She did not only listen to his words but the passion in his voice and was taken with him more with every word. They walked hand in hand around the village, looking at so much, what they didn't see was a shadow watching them.

Rayan walked D'Iyla back to the market so she could ride home with family. When they were within sight of the booth, they stopped. Rayan squeezed her hand gently, released it, and caressed her cheek again. "Tomorrow" he asked?

"There is nowhere else I would rather be."

He turned and walked away while she joined

her family.

Later, as D'Iyla was attending the sirins, the barn door opened.

"D'Iyla, we need to talk. Come sit with me." Her mother sat on a hay bale and patted the empty spot beside her.

"Yes, Boulo, what is it?"

"Who were you with today?"

D'Iyla stammered, "a new friend."

"I do not think that is wise. You need to keep your thoughts on the prince and your new life."

D'Iyla sighed heavily and looked down at the ground. It's not like she had forgotten about the agreement, but the time with Rayan had made it seem not real, like a story she read and could just file away on a shelf.

"I don't know who he is, but you need to stop seeing him and think about your family."

"But, Boulo, I…"

"No! Put aside any silly feelings you have. This is what's best for you."

Without waiting for an answer from D'Iyla, her mother stood up and left her alone in the barn. Tears sprung to her eyes and started to roll down her cheeks. "What am I to do now?" she asked herself and the sirin. Is there still a choice here? Can I answer my heart or follow my family's wishes? How could she tell Rayan, and how will he react?

D'Iyla sat in the barn, thinking and crying until

the animals were asleep and her eyes were red and puffy. She went to bed but did not sleep well.

There was a quiet knock on her door that woke D'Iyla. "It's late, you need to get up," her mother said gently entering her room. "Your chores are done already but you need to get ready."

"Yes, Boulo."

"I have made you something," her mother replied, holding up a new wrap. It was a plain royal blue, but she had sewn in silver beads which flashed in the light.

"It is beautiful!" D'Iyla sat up, rubbing her eyes.

"It's for the meeting today." She laid it down on the bed. "I will let you get ready."

The day was just starting but D'Iyla already felt exhausted and not ready to face it at all.

The hover cart was a little emptier now that they dropped her brothers to attend the booth while her parents and grandparents escorted her to the palace.

Along with her new wrap, D'Iyla was wearing a white skirt and a sheer white scarf covering her face except for her eyes. It was a protocol at the palace for unmarried women to hide their faces.

D'Iyla watched the palace grow larger and more daunting as they got closer. The palace and the surrounding grounds were beautiful, but D'Iyla couldn't see it past her feelings of sadness.

They were admitted through the gate and ushered into the palace. They walked in the front door and were directed to sit in a lush sitting room to the right. D'Iyla stood there, taking in the grand room. She had never even dreamed such luxury existed. All the furniture was upholstered in white cotton with pillows scattered around. The window coverings looked like white silk and there was a large white fur rug of an animal she couldn't identify that lay in front of the largest fireplace she had ever seen.

They were offered tea and asked to sit on the closest couch. Her family had arrived promptly but were kept waiting for almost an hour. D'Iyla's heart seemed to slink deeper into her body with every passing minute. Just when she thought she could wait no further, the far door opened. D'Iyla and her family rose to their feet. The start of a long procession of guards, councilmen, the prince's family, and the King and Queen marched in. Lastly, the prince strode into the room, wearing a royal blue tunic, matching D'Iyla's. D'Iyla and her family bowed deeply to the prince and his family. They sat opposite them.

Introductions were made all around, more for D'Iyla's benefit as her family had met everyone before. She nodded acknowledgement to everyone, not really knowing what to say or do. She watched the prince. His hair was slicked back, not one hair out of place. He had on multiple rings and had one jeweled earring in his left ear. His clothing was pressed and even his cologne smelled lavish. Grandfather was right, he did seem charming and smiled at her. He seemed totally at ease, like meeting a stranger who was to be his bride was an everyday occurrence.

There was a ritual to the meeting, and it started with a reading of the agreement. Each family was asked and consented to all the additions and changes. D'Iyla nor the prince spoke, but stared at each other. The prince sat back comfortably with his legs crossed while D'Iyla sat at the edge of the couch, her back aching from keeping her posture straight, trying hard not to fidget with her hands.

After the agreement was read, each family's lineage was also read aloud. D'Iyla was trying hard to pay attention; she knew this was important but all she wanted was to get out.

Finally, the ritual was done, everything was read. Now it was time to socialize and try to get to know her new family. The queen walked over to D'Iyla, her mother and grandmother joined them. The women bowed to the queen. D'Iyla gripped her hands tightly together. They briefly discussed the bonding ceremony. There was a strict protocol for it too, but a few things could be customized if D'Iyla wished. The queen beckoned one of her attendants over whom would help with the planning. It seemed the queen's part was done, and she walked away, letting her attendant take over the conversation. All D'Iyla could do was listen and nod. Her mind was in no state to help with the plans, and her heart ached for Rayan.

"This may be a little overwhelming for her right now. Can we think about all of this and contact you later," her mother asked the attendant.

"Of course." She bowed and backed up to rejoin the ranks of attendants and aides.

D'Iyla felt as though she might faint and was going to sit back down on the couch but then the prince stepped up and took her arm.

"Please, won't you excuse us a moment," he said to her mother and grandmother.

They both bowed and the prince led her to an unoccupied corner of the room.

"It's my pleasure to meet you" D'Iyla said, bowing.

"Of course, it is."

She looked at him, not sure what else to say. As she looked into his eyes, she was trying to see if they revealed anything about him, but his glare just sent a shiver through her.

"We have lots of time to get to know each other but I want to share a few things about myself. I am a proud man; I always get what I want, and I can be quick to anger."

D'Iyla continued to stare at him, growing more uncomfortable with every word. The prince was smiling as he spoke softly. Anyone watching would say he was professing his undying love to her.

"Furthermore, I am not happy with your choice of company lately. Rayan and his brother made me look like a fool. He is not a friend of your new family, and you need to stay away from him. You wouldn't want any harm to come to him, would you?"

D'Iyla couldn't speak, she just shook her head.

"And you don't want to see me unhappy now do you?"

She shook her head again. "May I at least tell him goodbye?"

"Yes, I will permit that. Is there anything else we need to discuss? Any other questions?"

"No," she whispered.

With all the charm he could muster, the prince bowed deeply to D'Iyla, stood, took her hand, raised it to his lips, and kissed it. Everyone in the room must have been watching them and their seemingly sweet exchange as they burst into applause for the couple.

The meeting ended shortly after, but it was not quick enough for D'Iyla. She rode in front of the hover cart home so she wouldn't have to see the palace as they left. Her grandmother chatted away the whole way home and commented on everything that happened.

"What did you two talk about?"

D'Iyla glanced at her grandfather who reached over and gently squeezed her knee. "Just getting to know one another."

"Well, we need to get changed and get back to the market quickly."

D'Iyla nodded. Her head was reeling, and her heart felt heavy. Too many questions swirled in her head. Does she go through with this? Could she even back out now? And her biggest fear, what will she tell Rayan? If she marries the prince, she will be protecting Rayan and her family but probably condemn herself to a life of fear and unhappiness.

The women returned to the booth after the midday meal and took over for her brothers.

"Oh D'Iyla," her brother Aadi called out. "There was someone who stopped by looking for you. He left you that." He pointed.

D'Iyla went over to the table where he pointed and there lay a trifollium. She wrapped her hand around it gently and brought it to her nose to smell. The instant she did, tears leaked from her eyes. She kept silent the rest of the day, working without thinking, numb to everything around her.

Later, she only picked at the food in front of her. The rest of the family discussed the meeting. D'Iyla excused herself early, finished her chores, and went to bed, never being so exhausted in her life. She slept uneasily, dreaming of searching for but not finding Rayan and being chased by shadows.

The next day, the market was closed, as it was once a week. There was much to keep her busy on the farm, housework to be done and their own pantry shelves needing to be filled for the upcoming cold season. It seemed they worked harder on their day off than any other during the week. D'Iyla's hands were kept busy but her thoughts were of Rayan, good thoughts and ones of worry.

The following morning at the market flew by. D'Iyla was more quiet than usual. Her mother and grandmother assumed it was the upcoming ceremony and plans but D'Iyla's mind was full of Rayan. She couldn't wait to see him but was dreading it at the same time.

At the noon break, she left for the park, without a lunch, her stomach too upset to eat. She walked slow. She knew what she had to tell him, she just didn't want to. D'Iyla kept glancing over her shoulder, looking for one of the prince's men.

The meadow came into view, but Rayan wasn't there. She stood there staring down at the river, trying to calm her mind and heart.

"I missed you the past two days," his voice sounded out behind her.

D'Iyla knew he was smiling, heard it in his voice, all the while she was fighting back her tears. She turned to face him as they escaped out of her eyes. His smile was quickly replaced with concern and worry.

"What's wrong?"

"I can't see you anymore."

"What? I don't understand."

She reached for his hands and pressed a note into them. "I just can't see you," she repeated. She squeezed his hand and walked past him, back to the market.

Rayan was stunned and confused and turned to watch her walk away. His hand gripped the note which sparked his brain back into focus. He opened it, it read:

My Rayan, please meet me back here after the market closes and I will explain everything. This involves the prince, and I am afraid for your life so please hide in the trees. I am so sorry for all of this.
All my love,
D'Iyla

D'Iyla made her excuses why she wanted to walk home and went to the park after they left. She walked to the edge of the meadow near the trees but did not enter the woods. She was still worried she was being followed. She turned to look at the river and softly called out, "Rayan, are you there?"

"I am here. Are you ok?"

With more tears streaming down her face, she told him everything from the agreement to the meeting and the prince's warning. Not looking at him made it easier to speak. D'Iyla poured out her heart to him. She told him all her fears and then all she felt for him. "I love you, Rayan," she said finally, holding her breath for his response.

"Come to me."

D'Iyla looked for anyone else who might be around. When she was satisfied they were alone, she walked into the trees and into his open arms.

After holding her for several minutes, he backed up slightly to look at her. "Can you get out of the agreement?"

"I am not sure. I am so very afraid of what may happen to you and my family if I even tried. I don't know what to do."

"We will figure something out together." He comforted her, pulling her close to him again.

Rayan walked D'Iyla part of the way home, only as far as the woods went, talking the whole time. "Meet me tomorrow at our normal time, near the woods again."

"Okay," she replied, staring up at him. Her head and heart, still so full of worry, were preventing any smile from forming on her lips. Rayan leaned over and kissed her gently. When he pulled away, her smile had returned.

At noon the next day, D'Iyla made her way to the park, again, watching for anyone following her. She sat down on the grass but didn't have to wait long.

"I'm here my love."

Her heart skipped a beat.

"Are you serious about not going through with this?" he asked.

"I want to be with you!"

"Would you be willing to leave here, your home?"

"Yes."

"Even if it may mean never seeing your family again?"

D'Iyla swallowed hard and took a breath. "I choose you!"

"I need to make some arrangements of my own, but I have a plan." He laid out the basic idea to her. "It's going to be risky, but I have many friends who can help. I will come for you in two days, after dark."

D'Iyla walked back to work in a sea of emotions. Her new life was racing toward her, and thankfully not the arranged one she had been dreading.

D'Iyla treated the next two days as though they were the last in her life. To some extent, they were. An end to her old life. She spent all her time with her family. She told them each how much she loved them in her actions. She also had to act like nothing had changed, that she would be marrying the prince.

The suns finally set and fell below the horizon; tonight was the night. She kissed her parents and grandparents good night, like she did when she was little. She went up to her room, appearing as though she was going to bed. She set out the small bag she packed. D'Iyla wasn't sure what to expect and had packed a few clothes, her knife, a little food, and a few sentimental things. She turned out the light and waited for the rest of the house to go to bed.

About an hour later, the place was quiet and D'Iyla grabbed her bag, imitated the sound, and snuck out to the barn.

"Rayan," she whispered.

"I'm here, my love," he whispered back. He came to her, kissed her gently, and pulled her in his embrace. "We have to go a little distance, can we borrow one of the arions?"

"Oh yes! Let's take Eous."

The steed was tall enough they needed a stool to climb on and wide enough that when they hung their legs down, their feet didn't even reach halfway down his belly. D'Iyla sat behind Rayan and put her arm around his waist. She had been riding Eous all her life and didn't need to hang on, she just wanted to be close to Rayan.

The moon was full, and was bright enough to light their way. Their own shadows stretched out behind them. They made their way quickly. Rayan knew the way but D'Iyla had never been so far from home before. He stopped Eous at the edge of the forest they came to. They slipped off Eous' back and led him into the forest. After a short walk, they came to a small vine covered mound. Rayan tied Eous to a nearby tree and approached the mound. He pulled on a thick branch attached to the mound and a door slid open.

"Do you hear that?" Rayan asked D'Iyla.

She stood still for a moment and the noise got louder. Twigs were snapping from the way they came.

"Hurry! We have been followed." Rayan opened the door and nudged her in. He followed her in and shut the door quickly and quietly behind them.

The hallway they stepped into was pitch dark, but a light appeared at the end and was coming towards them. D'Iyla clutched his arm and moved closer to him.

"Don't worry. They are all friends here."

"Rayan, bar the door and come in." A lady was carrying the light, coming towards them.

"Our steed is out there but we were followed. Jayzea, this is D'Iyla."

"Pleased to meet you" she bowed to D'Iyla.

D'Iyla bowed back.

"I will have Ojas take care of it."

They followed Jayzea down the hall which led them down underground. Soon the hallway opened up into a large, brightly lit room. There were dining tables in one corner and a few couches and chairs in another. There were a few people waiting for them. Jayzea went to find Ojas.

Rayan turned to D'Iyla. "We will sleep here tonight and leave close to dark tomorrow."

D'Iyla was tired for sure but didn't know if she

could sleep. She nodded at him.

"It's okay, we are safe here," he reassured her. He took her to a small bedroom that had several bunks. "Lay down and try to get some sleep. I am going to make sure everything is going as planned and will be back soon."

D'Iyla put her bag under a bed, sat down and removed her boots. Fully clothed, she laid down on her side, clutching the pillow under her head with one arm and hugging herself with the other. She laid there listening and waiting for Rayan to return. She dozed after a while but was gently awakened to Rayan laying down beside her, wrapping a protective arm around her. She pulled his arm closer, exhaled all her troubles, and fell peacefully asleep.

D'Iyla slowly awakened to quiet noises coming from the common room outside the bedroom door and from Rayan snoring softly beside her. She didn't move a muscle. She loved being this close to him. It just felt natural, and right where she should be.

"Rayan," a soft male voice came through the cracked door.

D'Iyla rolled over to face Rayan, and his eyes opened slowly. He saw her and smiled. "Bon dia."

"Bon dia," she smiled back. "Someone is looking

for you."

Rayan turned over to see who was in the doorway and turned back toward her. "I think it's time to get up." He winked at her, got out of bed, and waited for her. He opened the door and they stepped out into the common room. There were more people than last night when they came in. They were at the tables, talking and eating. Rayan introduced her to everyone and then found them spots to sit. Dishes of food were passed around. D'Iyla didn't realize how hungry she was until she smelled the first bowl handed to her.

When they were almost done, excited voices carried down from the hallway they came down the night before. A small group of people walked into view. D'Iyla looked up from her plate and recognized a face. "Tata, is that you?" She ran over to him and hugged him. "What are you doing here?"

"We have much to discuss Navasi. Sit back down."

Everyone sat except for her grandfather. He started to speak to the crowd but again mostly for D'Iyla's benefit.

"We are the Order of Rama, god of virtue, and help those who need it." He removed his leather bracelet from his wrist and held it up. Everyone else, including Rayan raised up their arms. D'Iyla could see a tattoo on her grandfather's arm which matched everyone else's, including Rayan. "That's your secret?" she asked Rayan. He nodded. "Guess a few of you have secrets," she turned to face her grandfather again.

"The prince's guards are in the woods. I assume they are looking for you Navasi. We need to adjust our plan."

The group discussed the situation for quite some time, everyone throwing in suggestions. Finally, a new plan was formed which everyone agreed upon, except for D'Iyla. The group split up, and her grandfather joined Rayan and D'Iyla. She looked at him. "How long have you known about us?"

"Rayan came to me after talking to you the first time in the booth after he figured out who you were. Rayan's father was a knight in the Order, and Rayan has had the rank of Ranger for almost a year. He is a very honorable man and has proved it time and again. I knew he would never hurt you. He came to me again after your discussion a few days ago, and I helped him plan this. You could have come to me, Navasi. I told you, I can help."

D'Iyla shook her head in disbelief. She had learned so much this week, so much has changed. "I do not like this plan. The time for me to be quiet about all that affects me is over."

"No one else is now planning your life for you, Navasi. We are just planning on how to get you to somewhere safe. You can make your own life once you get there."

D'Iyla looked at her grandfather, hesitated but nodded.

"Okay, it's settled then. We will wait until later to set this in motion." He turned to D'Iyla. "Your bracelet has our protection seal on it. There are houses of the Order all over the planet. They will help keep you safe."

"I don't want to put our family in danger," D'Iyla pleaded.

"Don't worry, Navasi. I will take care of them, and the Order will help me."

"I hate to leave you," she said with tears forming in her eyes.

"You must! This is the only way to get the life you deserve," her grandfather replied, taking her hand.

"Will I ever see you and the family again?"

"Let me worry about that too," he said as he gathered her in for one of his bear hugs. "I need to go back home now. I will take Eous with me."

D'Iyla reluctantly released her hold on him. She stood on her toes and kissed his cheek. "I love you."

"I love you too." He turned to Rayan. "Guard her with your life and love her with all your being."

"It will be an honor and my greatest pleasure." Rayan bowed deeply to him.

D'Iyla watched him leave. Rayan put his arm around her and pulled her close.

There wasn't much to do but wait. There was tension in the air as the day dragged on. Rayan talked her into laying down to rest, but she couldn't sleep knowing the obstacles in front of them.

"It's time, my love." Rayan sat beside her, caressing her arm. She got out of bed wordlessly and followed him through the common room and to the hallway.

"You remember where and when we will meet up?"

"Yes, but I have a little help. Jayzea gave me this." She held up a small device. "This will lead me there. She called it a Brujula."

"She is a smart and strong woman. You have a lot in common. She had an arrangement of her own but escaped the palace."

"I didn't know."

"She will guide you out."

"Please don't go or let me come with you. I don't want to be apart from you," D'Iyla grabbed his arm.

"I am the only one who can draw the guards off so you can get away. I am a Ranger. I have been training for this my whole life. Trust me, my love! They won't be able to keep me from you!"

He kissed her with a fire and passion that gave them both strength and faith. He backed away slowly from her, each of them not wanting to lose sight of the other.

D'Iyla felt more alone than she had ever in her life. She fought the tears. She needed to be strong for Rayan.

When it was time for her to go, Jayzea came for her. "Do you have everything?"

"Yes, and this" D'Iyla held up the Brujula.

Jayzea led her the opposite way they came in and took her deeper underground to another door leading her out. She stopped D'Iyla and motioned for her to be quiet. "Wait here," she whispered. She opened the door quietly and stepped out into the darkening day but returned quickly. "It's time. Let me turn it on for you." She took the device from D'Iyla and flipped a switch on the side. The dial on the front lit up dimly and it came to life. "The arrow shows you which direction to head and will turn from yellow to red when you get close. A few of us will be out there running interference and being decoys. Be as quiet as you can and don't stop."

"How can I ever thank you?"

"Rayan helped me when I needed it most. I owe him my life."

D'Iyla hugged her, kissed her cheek, and crept off into the woods.

"Rayan, where are you"?

D'Iyla glanced at the horizon again, glad the darkness was fading but her worry remained. There was a rustle of bushes behind her. She drew her knife and turned to face the path again. She held her breath but released it quickly as she saw Rayan run towards her. She sheathed her knife and held out her arms. He slowed slightly but rushed at her, picking her up and swinging her around. He set her down, cupped her face with his hands and kissed her.

"We need to get moving. The Prince and his men aren't too far behind." Rayan grabbed her hand, and they ran up the hill. The path led them to the top and fifty yards away was a transport ship.

The voices were faint but catching up to them. "We need to run faster," Rayan urged her. They ran towards the ship but as they got there, Rayan pulled her around to the back side of it.

"What are you doing?"

"Trust me!"

He forced her to climb down the cliff face below the ship. They climbed quickly, stopped on a ledge, and he pulled her into a small dark cave right before the explosion.

Her gasp wasn't heard over the tremendous boom. The hill shuddered and tiny rocks and dust fell onto them.

Rayan covered her mouth with his hand, silently pleading with her to stay quiet. She grabbed his hand away, nodding. He led her back out of the cave and pointed down to the canyon floor. They didn't have much farther to go. Rayan knew with the fiery ship above, the prince and his men would figure they died in the blast and wouldn't be follow them into the canyon, but he didn't want to take any chances. They climbed down, hugging the canyon walls as they made their way to the woods beyond.

He let her rest once they were under cover of the trees. "We don't have much farther to go."

"Let's just get there," she urged.

They walked through the woods and came to a clearing and there sat another transport ship.

"Do we actually get to use this one?" D'Iyla asked.

"Well, we did use the last one, just not in the conventional way," he smiled.

They boarded the ship; Rayan went to go speak with the pilot, and D'Iyla found a seat facing a window. The stars were almost gone, one sun starting to present itself for the day. Rayan came and sat beside her.

"You were late, I was so worried!"

"I know, my love," he said, grabbing her hand. "I had to get this." Rayan reached into his jacket pocket and presented her with a trefollium.

She took it from him and breathed its scent in deep. She squeezed his hand and looked into the sky as they raced towards their new life together.

About Pamela James

Pamela James has contributed short stories to the Anthologies of *Beneath the Twin Suns, In the Red Room* and *Star Crossed*. Those stories have been mixed with romance, sci-fi and mystery. She is writing a book that is crossed with action and romance but she hasn't picked one genre to write in exclusively. She doesn't have much to promote as of yet but watch out, she hopes to finish her book soon and share it with the world and has quite a few more ideas to turn into great stories.

Exiled
by D.W. Hitz

CHAPTER ONE

Keven emerged from the bizarre forest and gazed into a vast swamp. Bubbling gasses popped through the thin ooze that layered the water's surface. Each bubble's burst intensified the air's thick burnt-cinnamon stench. Small islands, a few yards wide, dotted the expanse and hosted muddy humps of dry grasses and scrubby bushes.

Hesitation weighed down Keven's legs. He didn't want to trudge through that. Life aboard a habitat in the center of a hollowed-out asteroid had been without such messes. He'd only read about wilderness and swamps in the archives. He'd never muddied his boots or splashed in unpurified water. But as a gentle wind blew through his hair, he was reminded that there may be a lot of things he'd have to deal with here that he didn't aboard the Lifeboat. There would be a lot of things yet to discover if he was to find Thela.

How could it all have gone so terribly wrong?

The crash replayed in his head. Navigation would have said a collision between the Lifeboat and this system's asteroids was a one-in-a-million chance, but now, here he was. An alien sky looked down on Keven. Pungent smells of extrinsic plants and swamp gasses filled his nose. Trees around the crash site resembled inverted octopuses more than they did plant life.

When he had first emerged from his crashed section of the habitat and saw an emerald glimmer in the atmosphere, he was briefly enamored with this world's beautiful abnormality. His elation was short-lived. He learned that when the Lifeboat split, Thela and M Section landed in different locations. The air's stiff scents overloaded his senses. His fellow survivors proved more constraining than helpful. His irritation bloomed.

Keven decided he should double-check his bearings before taking a muddy step into the swamp. "Cypher, verify the crash vector of M Section and overlay my course."

"Certainly," Cypher's stiff male voice responded. The AI suspended a cartographic hologram over the terrain ahead of Keven.

Keven studied the digital reconstruction above the horizon. The Lifeboat decoupled twenty-two habitats into discrete evacuation pods. The asteroid around them exploded into fiery rock that rained onto the planet. Pods and debris rolled and smashed into each other. Eight pods ruptured and exploded, becoming indistinguishable from the asteroid's ruins. Fourteen held their trajectories and crash-landed on the planet's surface.

A green line followed the path of pod B, leading back to Keven's crash site. A red line traced the course pod M had taken. The line arced across the sky's green shine, over the swamp, through more tentacled trees, and behind a small mountain.

Keven cringed at the reenactment's end. His eyes shut as he sighed. There was no way of knowing how pod M had handled its landing. It could have fired thrusters, and smoothed and stabilized its descent. It could have malfunctioned as his had and crushed its shell and half its passengers. Or, it could have slammed into one of those mountains and disintegrated instantly.

"No," Keven muttered. "She's okay. I know it." The words of his pod-mates rang in his ears. They called him crazy. They begged him to stop. But he had to keep going. He had to find her.

Cypher drew a yellow line across the world in front of Keven. It bisected the swamp, taking him through the trees and over the mountain.

"I'm afraid that is the best route I can give you at this time," Cypher said. "The interference in this planet's atmosphere has not decreased, and I'm still unable to contact any evacuation pods or properly scan the surface beyond the visible spectrum."

"It's good enough, Cypher."

Keven looked back at the things he could only loosely describe as trees. Their upward-pointing tentacles waved in the breeze. He looked along the ground, hoping to find a stick or something to test the swamp's depth and consistency. Nothing.

"I guess I have to do this the old-fashioned way."

Keven extended his leg, setting one foot into the mud that lined the swamp's shore. As his boot sunk in search of a solid surface to hold his weight, Keven was grateful that he was wearing an environmental suit. He hadn't needed to activate his helmet yet, but he was sure the bio-shields in his suit's lining were in for a test by the bacteria living in the muck ahead.

Once it had reached a dozen centimeters deep, Keven's foot found enough firmness to hold his weight. He sighed and swung his other foot into the mud. The same dozen centimeters compacted under his weight, and he paused.

"No going back now."

Keven pushed on into the swamp, nine more paces before he was walking in slimy water, and the thick greasy muck was up to his knees. Bubbles popped around him. Mud slurped with each step, its suction clinging to Keven's boots. Yellow and green water splashed and trickled back down. He grimaced and kept going, fighting for every foot he gained.

Eventually, Keven's trail through the swamp became level. He wasn't sinking any lower. With the path evened out, and the distance to travel great, Keven's mind wandered to the monotonous squish, splash, slurp of his journey.

He found himself remembering the past, when he had gone up and explored the surface of the asteroid with Thela and her brother, Palon. The Lifeboat had passed through a small nebula, and someone said it was as blue as the earth's sky once was. Thela had to see it.

She grabbed Keven in one hand and her brother in the other, and dragged them both to the airlocks. She pushed and teased and charmed them both until everyone put on EVA suits and sneaked out of the Lifeboat.

Standing on the surface of that asteroid and staring off into the abyss of space was the most humbling, terrifying, and thrilling experience of his life. He stared through the sky-blue energized hydrogen in wordless awe, while knowing that a single misstep may send him off to spend the rest of his life in that nebula. But her hand was holding on to his. Thela's grip on his right hand grounded him like a titanium chain and quelled his bubbling fear.

Keven found himself nearing a mound of mud, a several-meter-wide island. He aimed for it. After almost an hour of walking, his feet and legs were burning and needed the rest.

He was almost there. The ground inclined upward, and something brushed against his leg.

"What the..." Keven halted. His gaze swept the water around him. Nothing was moving. Nothing caused waves other than his own legs. Maybe he imagined it. Cypher had said that the existence of animal life on this planet was improbable, after all. He continued toward the island. He needed to get there, to stop and rest.

Keven pulled himself onto the dirt mound one heavy foot at a time, and then dropped to his knees, then his rear.

"I can't believe I'm doing this." His boots held more dirt than he had witnessed in his entire life. He'd covered more distance since the crash than he walked in a week on the Lifeboat. Keven stretched his legs out in front of him and leaned back. His thighs and calves were burning and throbbing. None of his low-G exercise regimens prepared him for this.

The way ahead was long. Keven looked at the forest beyond the remainder of the swamp. He glanced back to see the distance he had traveled. As tired as his legs were from trudging through that swamp, Keven was starting to wonder if he could make it through the rest. His thoughts went to Thela. Was she okay? Could she be trying to find him? What if she was hurt and needed his help? He would have to make it.

"Cypher, do you have suggestions on how to get across this mess faster?"

"I have analyzed the consistency of the water and bio-matter your EVA suit has encountered. I can offer another strategy."

From Keven's belt, two nano-capsules popped up from holsters. Keven lifted the disks and held them up. "I didn't know this suit was equipped with nano-capsules."

"They are only authorized for emergency situations," Cypher said. "My programming has deemed this acceptable. The disks are ready. Set them in the water ahead of you."

"Okay." Keven leaned forward and did as the AI asked. As the nano-capsules touched the water's surface, they began a construction cycle. They widened as they grew, their active edges glowing orange while gray material extended outward. Their shapes started to look familiar. Like things Keven had seen in a History class years ago. When the cycles finished, there were two new items: a long sleek container, and a single pole with flat ends. "They used to call that a canoe, didn't they?"

"Kayak," Cypher said. "It should work somewhat better in this shallow water than a canoe."

"Why didn't you suggest this earlier?"

"You did not ask. My intrusion settings are scaled low."

Keven rolled his eyes. "For the remainder of this trip, Cypher, raise intrusion settings. If you have an idea that's going to save me hours of time or help me get to

Thela, I want to hear it."

"Affirmative."

Keven rested for a few more minutes. He picked up the paddle and climbed onto the kayak. His fingers clutched the edges of the craft as if his life depended on it. It rolled left and right as he moved around, trying to figure out how to balance on the wobbling thing. After centering himself and placing his rear into the depression that seemed sculpted for it, the kayak stabilized.

He pressed the paddle against the land and pushed himself away from his island. He then sloshed the flat end into the water and heaved, propelling himself forward. He switched to the other side. Keven was almost giddy. It was working. He was moving across the water and at double or triple the speed he had been previously.

Keven watched the waves ripple away from the craft as it glided, and something translucent shimmered below the surface.

CHAPTER TWO

Keven weaved his vessel through patches of aquatic grasses and between scattered mounds of mud. After two hours of paddling, he had traveled more than three-quarters of the way through the swamp. The muddy beach beyond the water was starting to look like a reachable destination.

He puffed and paddled, ignoring the burn in his arms and shoulders. His heavy breathing sucked so much of the local stench into his body that he was nearly immune to the rank odor.

Bit by bit, the day was waning. Cypher had analyzed the system's star, a bright red giant that was nearing the end of its life. He reported that full days would last nearly thirty hours, but with daylight for only eleven and extremely cold nights. The story was eerily similar to the Earth's final years, after the sun had begun burning helium and the planet's rotation slowed.

Now, with visible signs of daylight depleting, Keven felt a gnawing urge to get to the end of this swamp and find cover for the night. He slammed the paddle into the water and forced his tired arms to push faster.

Swamp spray splashed onto Keven's arms, chest, and neck. The water was cool, but his suit rubbed against his scrapes from the crash. The fabric was designed not to chafe, but after hours of use, it still irritated. He grunted and paddled again, this time splashing himself on the cheeks, nose, and getting drops in his right eye.

"Ugh," Keven stopped. He hissed, as the corner of his eye burned. He closed and rubbed it. "Dammit." The burn spiked, and Keven flexed his muscles, trying to distract himself from the pain. He breathed deep, and after a moment, the eye began to numb, and the burn lessened.

Keven shook his head and panted. "Have to make landfall. Don't want to spend the night out here."

He dipped his paddle back into the water. He pushed on his right, and the water felt strangely thicker. He switched to the left and paddled again. It felt normal. He switched again, and something firm thumped the bottom of the kayak. He hit something solid with the paddle.

"Now what?" Gazing down, nothing was around the vessel except empty swamp water. It looked waist-deep, and Keven could actually see the mud below the swampy sea. A chill ran down his back. "I don't get it."

Keven placed his paddle into the water, stabbing the muddy bottom. A cloud of dirt puffed up, and a shadow flashed across the murk.

Keven's pulse quickened. "What is that?"

He looked skyward. Could something above him have made that shadow? The sky was clear. He leaned over the edge of his craft and drew a circle in the water with his paddle. Ripples rode the tiny waves and gently stirred the mud below.

"I—must have imagined it." His heart thumped. He took a breath and sighed. "No animal life, remember. Keep moving."

Keven focused his sights on the shoreline ahead and continued paddling. The water was thick, but he ignored it. He had to keep moving. He strained. Left. Right. Left. Right. The burn returned to his forearms and then shoulders and back. He forced himself onward.

Eyes on the shore. Focus.

Minutes passed, the water was smoother, but the paddle had become heavier.

Focus on the shore. You're just tired. You can rest at the shore.

A coolness touched Keven's left hand. It felt nice. His EVA suit was supposed to relay temperature and texture to the user, though it just felt hot most times. This was nice. The splashing water was finally doing something helpful.

Left, right, he kept up his pace. The shore was closer, maybe a couple hundred meters.

The cool sensation traveled up Keven's arm. Was he really that wet? He had been tossing a lot of water, but should he be that wet?

Keven took his eyes off the shore, but kept paddling. He glanced at his left sleeve. There was wetness there. A substance that was thick, in a long line, slimy.

"What is that?" He stopped paddling. The kayak drifted slowly under its own momentum. "What did I splash myself with?"

He sat the paddle across the kayak and reached to touch the slime with his right hand. It was soft, cool. He pressed into it, testing its density.

The slime jerked. It shot up Keven's arm with a slurping and sloshing sound.

"What the hell?"

It heaved itself up to his bicep and rolled. Five translucent tentacles of slime shot from the object and grabbed Keven's shoulder, yanking it up higher.

It moved toward Keven's face. He tried to grab it. It slipped right through his fingers and slithered closer. An image crossed Keven's mind of this thing sliding right into his suit. What would it do then? He tried to grab it again. No luck. Its slimy arms reached for his face.

"No!"

The rim of Keven's EVA suit sprung up from behind his neck. It crossed over his head, flew down in front of his face, and slammed shut below his chin.

"Helmet activated," Cypher said. "I hope you don't mind me taking the liberty."

Slimy tentacles banged on the suit's transparent face shield. "Gah!" Keven shouted. The small translucent tendrils searched the contours of the shield, searching for a way inside. Trails of slime followed their writhing flux.

With two hands, Keven seized the thing and hurled it away into the water. He rubbed his hands together. They slipped along each other in the thing's emulsion. "What the hell was that?"

"I'm not sure," Cypher said. "I don't have records of any encounter with a creature like that. I would have to speculate—"

"Wait," Keven said. He felt a cool something on his cheek. Small and wet, like a drop of water. Instinctively his hand went to his face, but his helmet blocked it. The wet drop moved. It slid up his cheek. His hands searched furiously, trying to reach his face. "It's inside! Some got inside!"

The cool wetness traveled up Keven's left cheekbone. He could see it now. It was tiny, shiny, and stretching closer to his eye.

"Open the helmet!" Keven's face shield flipped up, and the tiny slime droplet slithered over Keven's eyelid and onto his eyeball. It stretched and slid across the surface of his eye, burning as it crawled. Keven blinked hard and shook his head. It wouldn't break free. He brought his hands toward his face, and it darted down into the corner of his eye socket. It was under his skin, inside him.

Keven growled. His gloved hands rubbed his face and felt around his eye.

"Get it out! Get it out!"

"I'm afraid that isn't possible here. The organism seems to have taken refuge inside you."

"What!" Keven continued to feel around his face. He pushed against the bottom of his eye, hoping the thing would pop out. Instead, he felt it squirm deeper into the socket. It wiggled around, underneath his eyeball, toward the center of his head.

"Get it out of me!"

"You would need a surgical bay. Keven, I am sorry, there is nothing to do."

Keven panted. His heart pounded. But he could no longer feel the slime.

"What's it doing? Scan me!"

The helmet flipped closed, and the inside of Keven's EVA suit flashed with the dull white light of a med scan.

"Well?"

"There is nothing on the scan."

"Nothing? What does that mean? Is it the atmosphere?"

"Insufficient data. It may be the environment, or it may be the creature's biology."

Keven took a deep breath. The sky was dimmer. He was still over a hundred meters from land. He looked at the water. More of those things could be in there.

A burst of rage rolled over Keven's being. There was no way to fix his problem. That thing was inside him, and there was nothing he could do. He grabbed the paddle. One thing he could do was get out of the damn swamp.

Keven regained his breath. "Okay. Keep moving."

He paddled. He watched the shoreline. He wanted to focus there, but his gaze refused to cooperate. His focus went to the trees, the kayak, the swamp, where he had tossed whatever that was. The paddle's blades rose and dove into the water, and Keven repeatedly checked for more clingers. He looked at the shore and scanned for anything weird there.

"You said no animal life, Cypher. Would you like to revise your statement?"

"My report said the probability of animal life was low."

Keven ground his teeth. "What do you call that thing back there?" he snapped. He knew the conversation wouldn't do any good. But it felt good.

"I can only speculate."

"Please, speculate!" His loudness vibrated his suit. His fingers clenched the paddle and flexed.

"The highest probability would be a silicon-based life form. It would seem to have been a heat-seeking invertebrate."

"Heat-seeking."

"It is a speculation."

Land was almost within reach. Water became more clear and shallowed. There was a small beach, followed by more octopus-trees. Keven wondered loudly, "Any ideas on land creatures? Should I expect any heat-seeking invertebrates to come after me in the dark?"

"It is a possibility."

"Great."

The sun touched the horizon as Keven landed on shore. He dragged the kayak onto the beach and debated on what he should do with it. He may need it on the way back, but he couldn't carry the thing through trees and over a mountain.

Keven towed the kayak and paddle up to the tree-line, setting it beside the first row of plants. "I guess this is where we part ways."

"Show me the route, Cypher," Kevin said.

A yellow line appeared over the forest floor, and Keven headed in. The tentacled limbs of the forest branches waved in the breeze, and Keven's thoughts went to the thing crawling inside him. He couldn't feel it anymore. He somewhat wished he could, and he would at least know where it was. "Cypher, so another med-scan."

The scan's light illuminated his path for a few seconds.

"No change," Cypher said.

Keven walked in the twilight and made it nearly a kilometer before the darkness and his exhaustion pleaded with him to stop. "Cypher, can you program a shelter?"

A capsule popped outward from Keven's holster. He tossed it into a small clearing, and it started a construction cycle. Keven couldn't see exactly what it was building, only the orange rim of its assembly edge.

"Cypher, Light."

A pair of white lights shone from Keven's collar-bones. He saw a dark gray dome, roughly a meter tall with an entrance panel in the front.

CHAPTER THREE

As tired as Keven was, he found it hard to sleep. It wasn't too cold, the combination of his shelter and EVA suite kept him comfortable. The structure had thermal insulation and something of a soft floor. But instead of sleep, his mind wanted to wander and worry.

Keven always wanted Thela by his side when he slept. Now, she was who knows where. She could have been fine, of course, but she could also have been pinned under a crashed pod and in need of help. Keven blocked out the worse thoughts from crossing his mind.

Then, there was that thing in his eye. That creeped him out more than he could explain. The first thing he did once inside his shelter was remove his gloves and search the tissue around his eye with his fingers. He glided his digits over and around his cheek and eyelid. He found nothing. Cypher suggested the thing may just die and get pushed out of his system on its own. That was a nice thought, but it wasn't something Keven really believed.

Why did they have to crash? Why didn't the pilots do a better job of steering the Lifeboat? Why couldn't they have shot their way through that debris field, and did they have to decouple the ship?

None of his thoughts had answers, only questions and mind-scratching anxiety.

Keven closed his eyes. They shot back open as a noise roused him from sleep. A kind of shuffling noise, a scratch on the wall of his shelter.

Keven waited. Listened for it to come again.

"Cypher?"

"Yes?"

"What was that?"

"Inconclusive evidence."

"Of course, there isn't enough evidence to say specifically. Whatever it was, something was out there. Any ideas if it was environmental, or animal?"

"Inconclusive evidence."

"Yeah, same here."

Keven's eyes were dry and heavy. He looked up and studied the roof of the shelter. The planet's three moons had risen, and while the composite roof was strong, it was also thin enough to allow light through. And with it, shadows of tentacle-like limbs dancing and threatening from the night beyond.

"I'm sure it was nothing," Keven said.

When Keven awoke, it was still night. Had it been five minutes? An hour? Three? The shadows of octopus branches swayed on the roof, and the entire day ran back through his mind. He needed to get up.

He pulled himself into a cross-legged seat and stretched. His muscles were still tired. His joints still ached and burned as he extended and retracted his limbs. But there was a tingle of adrenaline spinning through his veins, and he felt like he needed to start moving and make use of it.

"Cypher, how long until dawn?"

"Ten hours remain until sunrise."

Keven was surprised. He had managed to sleep through nearly half the night.

"What's the temp outside?"

"Currently it is negative nineteen degrees Celsius."

"How much would it drain my EVA to keep my temperature up out there?"

"Power should be sufficient to last until the next solar charge using climate controls and computing for ten hours."

Keven stretched again and began crawling to the structure's exit. "Alright, then let's go." His hand touched the hatch release, and his helmet closed over his face. There was just enough outside air across his skin to chill his lips before his face shield sealed and warm air circulated through his suit.

The forest felt more barren in the moonlight than it had in the day. There were trees, but they had no leaves.

There was nothing on the ground but dirt and short, thin patches of grass. Keven thought of the images of Earth's forests he had seen. The ground was covered by sticks, leaves, stones, and a thousand other things. This forest was deserted.

"Cypher, Light."

Keven's chest lit the space in front of him, and he began walking.

Keven hadn't traveled far before his head began to itch. It wasn't an itch on his face or in his hair. It was an itch inside, underneath his skin and bone. He felt it behind his cheekbone, below his eye, and he knew what it was.

The feeling pushed him to walk faster. Thela's pod was supposed to be within reach by midday, based on Cypher's calculations. But that was still almost ten hours away. He hoped, God he hoped, that it wasn't a crash. Maybe, just maybe, there was an intact medical bay in her pod, and they could get this thing out of his head.

Keven wondered as he walked. Were there any medical personnel in M Section? Sure, an AI could do most medical tasks, but having a real human in charge, that's what he really wanted. But the whole thing happened so fast. Anyone could have been in that section when the Lifeboat decoupled. Nothing broke up as it was supposed to. Neither supplies nor weapons were distributed to sections before they split. Keven growled as he thought about whoever was responsible for the decoupling procedure.

The ground was getting brighter, and Keven looked up into the heavens. It wasn't a premature sunrise, but another moon — a big one.

"Cypher, I thought there were only three moons."

"It would appear that data was false."

"Really?" Keven shook his head. "How do we have such bad data? You said there was no life here. We found life. You said three moons. That is a fourth moon. What's next? Has the air I've been breathing on this planet contained cyanide?"

"At most, minimal traces."

"What?"

"Cyanide is being released by the tall structures all around us. But the concentration is extremely low."

"Forget I asked, Cypher."

In the bright light of the fourth moon, Keven noticed a shine on the trunks of the octo-trees. They ran up from the ground in lines that traveled into the branches like glowing pinstripes. But the tips of the branches glowed the most. The stripes merged there in solid bulges that appeared like they were opening toward the moon.

"That can't be," Keven said.

But it was true. As he kept walking, he saw the ends of the plants' tentacle-like branches split. They opened like flowers, like moon-blooming petals, spreading to absorb whatever special light this moon had to offer.

"Amazing."

The ground inclined, gradually at first, and then steeply. Keven had pushed himself as far as the mountain, and his mouth was dry under his heavy breath.

"Keven," Cypher said, "your vitamin and hydration levels are low. You should drink nutrimix soon."

"Yeah, I should." Keven hated the taste of EVA nutrimix, but he had come around to the fact that it was all he may have for a long time. It used the same process as the Lifeboat to recycle his lost water and add calories, vitamins, and minerals back into it. But the systems on the Lifeboat did such a better job of making it taste good.

A tube extended from the inside of the EVA suit's helmet to Keven's mouth, and he drank as he hiked up the increasing grade. Keven noticed that the itch inside his head seemed to lessen as he drank. By the time there was no more dryness in his mouth, and his energy was replenished with a belly full of carbohydrates, the itching sensation in his head had completely stopped.

"Does that mean it was thirsty too?" Keven said.

"Please repeat," Cypher said.

"Nothing."

Keven's eyes went back to the trees. Their bloomed tips had shifted. As the moon crossed the sky, the branches had tiled to follow it. They now pointed straight up and held open a larger bloom than before.

With the itch in his head subsided, anxious curiosity took hold of Keven's thoughts. "How does it do that?" He needed to know. He wasn't sure why he needed to know, but something compelled him.

He looked for a smaller tree, one with its bloom closer to the ground. He would take a moment to investigate, but didn't want to climb if he didn't need to. He looked, tree after tree, comparing heights. His pace became driven. After another twenty minutes down the path, Keven found one. While not quite a sapling, it was half the others' size, only three meters tall. A jolt ran through his fingers. He inhaled deeply.

Keven took hold of the tree, grabbing one of its branches and pulling it toward him. The limb was not as stiff as Keven expected. It bent with resistance, but didn't crack or break as wood might. It felt soft on the surface and harder within, and made Keven wonder what the structure of this plant looked like inside.

When Keven lowered the bloom enough to see inside it, he was speechless. While the branch had split and opened like a flower, there was no stamen or receptacle inside it. Instead, the glowing edges of the flower were spread into the mouth of a deep hole. Keven looked inside the plant, trying to see the bottom of the tube, and couldn't.

Anger flared in Keven's chest. He was unsure of where it came from, but it was pure and demanded addressing. Why couldn't he see what he expected? Why didn't this make sense? Why was this plant taunting him?

"Cypher, I need a cutting tool."

"What kind of cutting tool? There are many varieties."

"I don't know," Keven snapped. "Something to cut through this."

"Certainly." After a second, a nano-capsule popped on Keven's belt. "This should work."

Keven retrieved the capsule and held it in his open palm. An orange line led the construction cycle, and after several seconds Keven held a large black knife. Its handle fit his grip precisely and felt surprisingly good in his hand. Its blade was as long as Keven's forearm. "Yes, this should work."

He examined the blade and thought of Thela. She would like this blade. Isn't it beautiful? A brief doubt popped into his head. Should he be doing this? Shouldn't he be getting back to his mission? The question was purged from his mind as an overwhelming will pushed him back into the moment.

Keven pinched a single petal in his left hand and placed the edge of his blade between the bases of it and the next petal. He felt a trickle of adrenaline run through his veins. He was going to see inside this thing. He would see how deep that hole went, and maybe what was making this tree limb behave in such a strange way. The plant was going to share its secret, Keven had no doubt.

The blade bit into the tree's skin and split the limb with barely any pressure. The cut went down several dozen centimeters, and there was still no end in sight to the bottom of the bloom. Was the tree hollow all the way to its roots? No. Keven would find the end, find out why.

Keven pushed lower, cutting further. Translucent violet fluid seeped from the tree's split edges, and the ground below his feet began to vibrate.

CHAPTER FOUR

The limb in Kevin's hand jerked free and shot away. At once, all ten branches of the plant bent to the other side of its trunk. Keven took a step back, his mouth dropping wide. All ten limbs snapped toward him, striking him in the chest.

Keven grunted and soared backward. His EVA suit tightened and hardened as his back slammed into the trunk of another tree.

"What was that?"

The ground rumbled. Keven watched as the tree in front of him erupted from the soil. It grew upward, its trunk thickening as it rose. The trunk behind him rumbled and moved upward as well. The earth below Keven's feet cracked and crumbled. Dirt shook as the ground opened.

Keven scrambled to his feet and ran. Ahead, he saw the mountain's incline turn rocky, the end of the forest. He pumped his legs and heard crunching and grinding, roaring of the land beneath him. He glanced back as he moved.

Every tree for at least a kilometer was rising, moving as if with a singular mind. They breached the soil, and Keven saw that their bases were connected.

"Not a forest," Keven exhaled. It was a single entity, joined by tissues beneath the dirt. And it was rising in anger.

Keven screamed and propelled himself harder. The trees on his left and right rose. Twenty meters to the rocks, where crevices and cracks, large boulders could provide cover.

A loud whoosh of wind swelled into a roar. Keven could feel it moving in on him. Fifteen meters. The rows of trees in front of him rose.

Keven glanced back. A tidal wave of tentacle limbs folded forward and toward the ground. They slammed, lifting an enclosing wall of dust and pressure, and their destruction was cascading closer second by second.

Ten meters. Keven's throat burned. His legs were numb. He reached forward, wondering if he could possibly find safety in the rocks ahead, before the living trees of this horrible planet came down and crushed him to death.

He screamed. Five meters. The ground below his feet cracked. Thela smiled at him on the surface of that asteroid. Her eyes glistened in the starlight. Her dimples punctuated her exuberance. He remembered that smile. There was no reason for him to note it at the time. No reason to think it was significant of anything more than a single event in the infinite flow of trivial occurrences. But it hung in his mind like constellations in the sky, as he stretched each stride and thrust each pace. He had to move faster. He had to see her face once again.

Violet arm-like tissues rose above the planet's surface as Keven leaped the last meter. They jerked, ejecting from the ground and hooking onto Keven's foot. His hands grabbed for the stone ahead, but he was rocketed upward. The dark purple thing clung to his foot like the slime of that swamp organism, raising him above the rocks, holding him in place, as the wall of crushing limbs barreled closer.

Keven's arms flailed as he tried to grab hold of anything. He tried wiggling, squirming, dislodging himself from the giant purple thing, but he was stuck.

"Cypher," Keven called, "help!"

Keven felt a capsule pop from his holster.

"Build this beneath you," Cypher said.

Keven seized the capsule and slid it below his belly. It warmed, and he felt Cypher harden his EVA suit from his toes to his head. Between his body and the entity's tissue, a barrier inflated. It quickly formed an oval larger than Keven's body, prying him from the entity's grasp and sliding him away.

Keven felt weightless. His body fell from the rising mass of living plant-life toward the field of rock and boulders below. The thing had lifted him twenty meters into the air, and now he raced back down. He tried to move his hands in front of his face as stone closed in. He tried to rotate his body into a better position. His EVA suit wouldn't allow it. He would be frozen like a statue until Cypher released him.

"Cypher!" Keven called. Air felt thin inside his suit. His head collided with rock.

Keven's eyelids cracked open. He looked through fuzzy eyes and a foggy face shield. Rock walls surrounded him. The largest moon hung in the sky, obscured by rocky spires, and then was eclipsed by a rolling wall of darkness and noise.

The sky was a pale green. The stars of early morning faintly shined through.

Keven stretched his neck, leaning his head left and right. He laid on an incline, his head the lowest, his waist on the arch of a boulder, and his legs hanging from the other side. He didn't remember ever sleeping in such an odd position before. Had he fallen asleep like this?

No. The events of the night returned to him. The hike, the trees, the tsunami of living vengeance. He fought to sit up. He perched himself on the boulder and looked at the rock walls around him. Gray and red granite. They saved his life. Didn't they? "I'm alive. Right?"

Keven felt his body up and down. He was covered in a layer of dirt and pebbles, but otherwise okay.

"You are alive," Cypher said.

Keven climbed around the inside of his stone shelter and found his way out. The forest that had attacked him had returned to placidity, right where it had been before. Trees weren't hundreds of meters tall. They weren't moving, rolling, trying to kill him. Had that really happened?

The memory of running for his life filled his senses, and rage bubbled inside Keven's belly. He scanned the tops of the octo-trees. Still. Lifeless. The disgusting things watched and waited for the next time a traveler may do something they didn't like. Keven was overcome by the urge to go get fire and torch the entire thing. Burn the entire entity away so nothing would ever have to face what he did last night.

"Wait?" Keven said. "Why? Why am I so angry? I got away." His fingers curled inside his fists. "There's no need to destroy it now." But he wanted to. He felt his teeth clench.

"But they killed my family. They'll keep killing."

That wasn't right. The words left Keven's mouth, but where had they come from. His parents had been dead for years. Lost on another exoplanet that the Lifeboat passed before this one. It was an exploration mission. Where were those words coming from?

The sun was rising. Keven collapsed his helmet and felt a cold breeze. The trees barely moved.

"Evil things. We'll make them pay."

An image crossed Keven's mind. He saw an enormous violet creature deploy its roots and invade a swamp. Octo-trees sprang up there, draining the water, drying the mud. Hundreds of translucent slime creatures writhed in the sun, drying away into crusted shells.

That's a memory. That thing is in my mind.

"We'll kill it one day."

CHAPTER FIVE

Keven stopped and leaned against a boulder, catching his breath. He glanced at the way he had come. Down the mountain, over thousands of granite boulders, fissures, and spires, were a dozen kilometers he'd crossed. He'd hiked up, with nothing but time to think, and time to share thoughts with whatever this thing was inside his head.

He'd recited to himself how he and Thela met, working on the Command Crew of the bridge. He told the story of how Howard tried to get in the way, worm his way between their affections, and what he had to do to set things straight. He spoke as if to a human audience, feeling his words being absorbed by an alien one.

It was an intelligent being of some kind, he had decided that for sure. But it wasn't a full mind. Its thoughts and memories were fractured.

Keven couldn't tell if the memories and emotions he was being subjected to were segmented because the creature was dismembered back in the swamp. Or, perhaps the creature was part of a larger, collective consciousness. It seemed like it was binding with his own mind as if it had done so before.

Flashes of its memories came more often and more vividly. Images of the swamp, images of some underground place, and some bright location Keven couldn't identify. And headaches now circled his skull, with waves of new pain as each memory flowed in and out. Keven wasn't sure whether the cause was a weakness of the human mind to not be able to handle a collective connection, or the alien now drilling through his brain.

Beyond the pain, though, the raw emotion Keven was bombarded with was the more frightening matter. Anger, at a magnitude he had never felt, rushed through his thoughts. And sorrow, grief saturated Keven to his bones and made him tremble. On and off, the emotions switched. And each time, Keven either wanted to curl up and die, or slam his fists into the rocks. The fear of what this entity was doing to his mind constantly made him hate it and mourn for it.

Keven turned and looked up the mountain. "Cypher, show me the path again."

The yellow holographic line curved in and out of rock structures and ridges further up the mountain.

"How far now?" Keven continued his hike. "What's my ETA?" And when can I get this thing out?

"Three hours," Cypher said. "You are seventy-four percent finished climbing up the mountain."

"Not soon enough." His patience for shared memories waned with each one.

Keven gritted his teeth. His head throbbed. Another wave was coming. The bones in his skull felt like they were being cracked apart from the inside. A line burned from the back of his head, across its top, and down the center of his face. The core of Keven's brain warmed, and unfiltered rage rushed through his thoughts.

He hated the rocks. He hated the dirt under his feet. He hated the green shimmer of the sky above. He hated the feeling of the EVA suit against his bare skin as he moved. Each stride sliding its fabric along his arms, legs, belly, and back. His muscles tightened, and his fists clenched.

Keven screamed at the sorry excuse for a planet he was marooned on.

"Who's down there?" a man said. It was a gruff, older voice, and Keven hated the sound. "Hello?"

A jolt shot through Keven's system. That was a human, another survivor on this floating rock. His rage eased back, and his mind began to function once again.

"Hello," Keven said. He heard the sound of EVA boots sliding on dirt and loose pebbles. "I'm from the Lifeboat."

"Us too," the man said. The footsteps doubled.

Keven moved faster, weaving in and out of boulders, over the next rocky ridge. They couldn't be far. He had to get to them. "Where are you?"

"We're up the mountain," the man said, "not far. Keep coming."

Panic gripped Keven in his chest. Something warned him that he had to hurry, or he wouldn't reach them in time, for something... He had to get up there. He pondered the voice and realized it was one he recognized. But he couldn't put a face or a name on it.

"Who are you?" Keven said. "What section are you from?" He climbed a ledge and came face to face with a hidden fissure in the mountain. A sharp drop-off led to a black abyss inside the world. Keven wobbled between a fall backward down the hill or forward into the blackness.

"No, no," Keven mumbled.

A pair of hands grabbed Keven's left shoulder. Another grabbed his right. They drew him against the wall of the mountain, then up over the abyss. His heart slammed so fast inside his chest, it was more of a hum than a beat. The hands drew him higher, tighter, and over the crest of another ledge.

Keven found himself on his back, looking up at a man and a woman in EVA suits just like his own. They were older than him by twenty years. Their faces were familiar, so much so that Keven was ashamed to ask again what their names were. He should know their names. Why didn't he know them?

"That was close," The man said. Gray stubble lined his chin and cheeks but didn't deter a softness about his gentle expression. He extended a hand and pulled Keven up to his feet.

"Thank you," Keven said. He examined the man

and the woman again. Whispers in the rear of his mind told him who they were, but only through feelings, distant emotions. A fear of authority and a kindness of heart. "I'm sorry, I feel like we've met, but..."

The woman smiled and leaned in to hug Keven. No. That wasn't right. Keven stepped back before the embrace could succeed, and she stepped away, pinching her lips together.

"It's okay," the man said, "it's been a while. I'm Garrison." He gave Keven his hand to shake.

"Kate," the woman said. Her voice broke, and she stared down as she offered her hand.

Pain circled around Keven's head again. This time reaching into the middle of his brain and squeezing. It drove him to his knees and delivered images of space. They were dark, with stars and glowing streaks of light. Gasses flowed and twisted in arrays of mirrored grace. Despite the pain, the view was beautiful.

As the vision and its strain faded, Keven again saw Garrison and Kate standing over him. "I'm sorry. There's something in my head."

"What do you mean?" Garrison said.

Kate's eyes were shining with concern.

Keven climbed back to his feet. "I need a medical bay. I think I have a parasite in my brain. And I need to find Thela. Are you two from M Section?"

"No," Kate said. "We're from S Section."

Keven saw a Lifeboat cabin with robot toys and holograms of red and yellow plants. "I grew up in S

Section. Where did you land?"

"We don't remember," Garrison said. "We both woke up on this mountain."

"And your AI units," Keven said, "can they tell you anything?"

"They don't seem to be online," Kate said.

"Huh." Keven pointed to the ridge above them. "You should come with me then, M Section should have landed this way, and with your missing memory, you could have head trauma. You may be in need of a med bay as well."

Keven led Kate and Garrison up the mountain. He filled them in on his search for Thela, and his experiences so far on the planet. They praised his dedication and applauded his determination through the pain and the intruder's effects on his system. It was the type of praise he hadn't experienced in years. It was heart-warming, pleasing, reminding him of a feeling within a lost memory. And it began a streak of suspicion about the two lost strangers.

Keven stepped atop the granite mountain's peak, Kate and Garrison behind him. It was a flat, cracked plateau near the sky, a hundred meters wide. Another forest laid on the other side of the mountain. This one was indigo, with short, leaf-baring trees. A thin plume of smoke rose from something ahead.

"Is that them?" Keven moved faster, and his head ached with burning pains. They dug into his brain from a hundred sides of his skull. Anger flooded his senses.

"It has to be," he growled and ran.

At the edge of the plateau, Keven stopped and looked down. Below him was a dizzying drop, a sheer cliff with only jagged rocks underneath. After that was the forest. Why another forest? He hated that forest. There was a river. Why more water? His fists clenched as hard as they could. He felt his muscles pinch at their limits. Forest resumed, and a hundred meters in, there was a clearing. And in that clearing was a safely landed pod. M Section.

"They better have a med bay," Keven growled.

People walked around the clearing, too far to tell who was who, but one, Keven would recognize her from the end of the universe. There was Thela. Her walk, her mannerisms, her essence, he recognized it all. She was there, alive.

Keven wanted to be happy. But instead, the rage boiled. Why was she so far away? Why was she in the wrong section when it all happened? She would have to explain herself. She'd have to ask for forgiveness.

The sound of footfalls grated on Keven's ears, boots scraped against rock. The other two were behind Keven. He turned, and their faces were blank. Their eyes were glossed over in white, dead. Their hands were forward and flat, and he saw their intentions. They were going to push him off the cliff.

"No!" Keven shouted. He grabbed Garrison's hand and yanked on it. He spun the old man in a wide half-circle and threw him over the edge.

A scream echoed, down and down.

Keven grabbed Kate. Her teeth glistened with drool. A growl escaped her mouth, and Keven spun her around, tossing her at the edge.

A smile crossed Keven's lips as Kate sailed over the rock. For a split-second, her fall seemed to pause, and her face shifted. She didn't have white eyes, they were blue and tearing. Her mouth screamed. And Keven recognized her. She was his mother.

"No!" Keven rushed to the ledge. He was too slow. He knew he was too slow. He would never catch her. His arm extended, and he reached out as she passed out of sight, below the cliff.

Keven stopped at the precipice and stared down. His body wobbled with an uneven weight.

No, it couldn't have been her.

Rocks shifted under Keven's feet. Pressure lowered onto his back. "No, no!" his arms shot outward and waved. He tried to regain his balance. The ledge slid out from under his boots, and he soared downward.

CHAPTER SIX

Captain Thela heard screams from a distance. On the mountain, she spotted a falling man.

"Howie," she said.

The Commander stepped closer.

"Someone just fell off that cliff," Thela said. "Get a crew member over there to help."

"None of our people are over there, Captain."

"Well, it looked human. It may be a survivor from another section, looking for help."

"Yes, Captain." Commander Howard set off.

"Captain," Lucia called from the edge of the pod. "Communications are up."

Thela watched the cliffs a moment longer. There was a nagging in her gut as she studied the rock.

"Captain!" Lucia called. "Section B, they have an urgent message."

Thela broke her gaze and strode back to the pod. She ducked under the open emergency hatch and climbed inside the habitat. She stepped right, to the command console and Lucia.

Lucia tapped the blinking red controls on the console. "It's an emergency recording."

"Play it," the Captain said.

Lucia pressed the playback controls, but nothing played. Her console's image phased out and back in. She tapped the recording again, and a spark shot from the side of the console. "Just a second, Captain."

The Comm Chief slid from her seat onto the floor. She opened the panel and began working inside layers of dense conduit.

Thela watched her officer, and the nagging in her gut churned. Something wasn't right here — something beyond the Lifeboat's sabotage and crash on this alien rock.

The communication console lit up, and Lucia climbed back onto her seat. "This should do it." She tapped the recording again.

"He escaped," Commander Cale's voice came through the comm system. It was rough, throaty. She continued, "The prisoner escaped. He killed five of us. He's headed in your direction, Captain." Gargled breaths and climate system hisses took over the recording.

"That's it," Lucia said. "It stops there. You don't think she means Lt. Drake?"

"I think that's exactly who she means." Thela turned and sprinted to the hatch. She jumped through and shouted, "Howie!"

There was no response from Howie.

Thela looked around and saw only her youngest cadet. "You, Briggs, where is Commander Howard?"

"He took Cole and Merkel and went into the forest. He said there was someone in need of rescue?"

"Dammit." Thela popped back into the pod. She opened the security storage, grabbing a stun rifle. She dropped back out of the pod and ran into the forest.

"Howie," Thela shouted. If only the comm system hadn't been destroyed in the crash... She had to catch up to him. He had no idea what he was walking into. It looked like whoever fell was wearing an EVA suit, so even a fall like that was survivable. "Howie," she shouted again.

She remembered Lt. Drake's trial, how he had sat with a lecherous grin aimed at her the entire time. They had gone on a single date, a mistake, where his delusions quickly surfaced. He had killed three people after she rejected him, and now he was on the loose.

"Howie," Thela shouted. She broke through the edge of the forest, finding the river. Chills crept over her skin as she saw the riverbank and Cole and Merkel on the ground beside it. Blood drenched their uniforms. It dripped slowly from long gashes in their necks. Commander Howard was on his knees. A deep laceration ran down his side, and the tip of a nano-capsule sword hovered in front of his chest.

"Keven, don't!" Thela said.

Lt. Drake was soaked from river water. His hair dripped, and his face twitched. He stared down the black blade of his sword into Howie's eyes.

"This is the reason, isn't it?" Drake said. His voice was dry and strained. "You've been cheating on me, with him."

Thela paused. What to do? She could try to shoot him, but she may not be fast enough. She could argue, but reason hadn't reached Drake in ages. All she could think was to play along. Maybe that would get Howie out alive. God, Howie. She trembled, thinking of Howie being hurt, dying. She wished they were back in bed before the alarms went off and this whole damned nightmare began. She breathed and steadied herself.

"I swear," Thela said, "I haven't been cheating on you. Howie's even said — we should be trying to get you out of that cell so you and I can be together."

"You're lying," Drake shouted. "You and your commander, spending all that time together. I know what you've been doing!"

Thela stepped toward Drake. "Just come with me. We can get through this. There's no more Lifeboat. It's just us." She waved him to come. She smiled as much as she could. Walk away. Get away from Howie.

Drake's face twitched. His eyes rolled in their sockets, and his free hand slapped his head. "Goddammit!"

Thela swung her rifle up and aimed it. Squeezed its trigger.

Drake's eyes opened with bloodshot rage as a wave of energy slammed into his side. It knocked him to the ground, and Howie too.

Commander Howard's eyes shut, he was out. Drake rolled over and swung his sword, slicing into the Commander's neck. His suit had absorbed the entire blast, and now his blade cut through the officer like slicing through air. Blood gushed onto the riverbank, and Thela screamed.

Drake howled and turned his sights to Thela. "I need your help." He rose and stumbled toward the Captain, crossing half the space between them. "There's something — it's in my head."

Tears streamed down Thela's face. She couldn't take her eyes from Howie's body. Blood washed over the riverbank, joining the quick-moving water and swirling into the current.

"It's some kind of alien," Drake said. His head leaned down, and a grin slid across his mouth. "It's inside my brain."

Thela refused to take her eyes from Howie. Maybe it wasn't as bad as it looked, and he would get up. Maybe he didn't lose as much blood as it seemed. But he wasn't moving.

The Captain's heart swelled with sorrow. Why did she send him off? Why did they have to crash? Why didn't they stay in bed and die together with the rest of J Section?

Something told her not to look up. If she did, there would be no turning back. There would be no chance that this was all a misunderstanding, and Howie couldn't rise sporting his trademark goofy smile and tell her it was all one of his pranks. Instead, this moment would be set, stamped into the fabric of reality. A concrete event, and there would be no undoing it.

Drake stepped closer. He raised his sword.

Thela looked down at her stun rifle and pinched the safety until it released.

Drake's sword tore through the air.

Thela placed the muzzle of her weapon in front of Drake's face and fired.

About D.W. Hitz

D.W. Hitz lives in Montana, where the inspiring scenery functions as a background character in his work. He enjoys writing in the genres of Horror, Supernatural/ Paranormal Thriller, and Science Fiction/Fantasy. He aspires to tell stories that thrill the heart and stimulate the imagination. When not writing, D.W. enjoys spending time with his family, hiking, camping, and playing with the dogs.

Find out more about D.W. Hitz below.

Website: dwhitz.com

Twitter: @dustinhitz

Branded
by Renée Gendron

Sergeant Major Emerlynne Turner of the Diplomatic Corps, watched the Jubliee's docking clamps secure to Archimedes Station. Thirty years ago, when Archimedes was built, it had been an architectural marvel. Six massive, curved pylons attached by transport tubes and walkways nestled in a nebula. Half a dozen metal prongs stretched towards the stars, reaching to a brighter future. Nestled on the edges of an asteroid belt long depleted of its biggest deposits, a steady but diminishing stream of income came from mining.

In the name of sectoral unity. The words were written in ten languages on each of the pillars. Emerlynne shook her head. Hollow words lost in the vacuum of space. Endless diplomatic bickering marred the quadrant leading to skirmishes, pirates, and threats of war.

"We're cleared to debark," the comms officer said.

Emerlynne straightened her dark-grey tunic, the one that took her years of twelve-hour a day training to earn. The docking bay door opened with a hiss. She pinched her nose and blew, but the change in air pressure still popped her ears.

"Do a sweep of the common areas," she told her team. "A pair to each pillar. Blend in." Not that she had to remind her agents. They'd worked as a team for five years, becoming better oiled and maintained than this bucket of bolts station.

She strode out of the polished corridors of the corvette straight out of space dock. The foul air of the station assaulted her nostrils. Sweaty stevedores manoeuvered heavy equipment, unloading and loading cargo. With both tongues hanging from his mouth and face dark blue from exertion, a Ulian stevedore dragged a metal crate across the bay.

Engines whirred and metal prongs grated against steel containers. A shower of sparks streamed from the cavernous ceiling. Two construction crews repaired a column damaged from a hovercraft impact.

Three people in filthy clothes lurked behind a cargo container. Emerlynne caught the eye of a man with platinum blond hair. His associates spotted their exchange and bolted for the exit.

Two of Emerlynne's agents moved to intercept them, but Emerlynne stayed them. "It's a petty drug deal. Don't chase them down but find out how they're smuggling goods onto the station."

"Ma'am." Spencer motioned for Dale and Winters to follow.

Emerlynne pushed her way through a crush of people buying passage off the station. Some wore fine wool clothing of the same fashion from Jenae Prime: striped three-button jackets with solid-coloured vests and matching trousers. Their overuse of cologne did nothing to mask the stench of elitism, dusty air, and desperation. Most wore workers' clothing, sullen colours with patches at the elbows and knees.

Emerlynne ignored the glowering looks from the people in the docking bay. The uniform. No one outside of the Core Sectors liked uniforms. The only time the edges saw them was to collect taxes, enforce the draft, or snap their necks.

Outside of the dock area, she took a shuttle to the administration pylon. Light-pink and rich blue gases caressed the domed ceiling of the shuttle. Half-way between pylons, she lifted off her seat. A warning light flashed, indicating they were out of the area of artificial gravity and would be so for another two minutes.

Floating. In a cloud. In space. A sense of serenity enveloped her.

The craft approached the administrative pylon and its gravity eased her down. Docked, the doors wheezed open and sweet air rushed in, pushing away the greasy smell of mechanical fluid and toil from the tube.

Bright and spacious, the docking area had a floor-to-ceiling map of the pylon. Three attendants in crisp green uniforms helped a knot Ellarians, their spring plumage sprouting, and Krusgens. Pale and squat, the Krusgens looked half-starved. A series of planet-wide windstorms devastated their crops, causing twenty percent of their population to seek refuge on other planets.

One of the administrative attendants raked his gaze over her, clutched his tablet to his chest, and went to her.

Junior Adjunct Jan Henni, said the nameplate on his chest. Polished to the point of brilliance. Did he put it on an altar each night and pray to it?

"Sergeant Major Turner, we weren't expecting you this soon." He hurried to her, the other two attendants in tow. "Chief Administrator Sauer is in meetings all afternoon, but I do have briefings for you."

She remained silent, waiting for an explanation with her best I'm-out-of-patience-stare.

"The stevedores are threatening to join the industrial action of the factory labourers. If we don't contain this situation..." The Ulian's face blanched from dark blue to light blue.

Procedures. Even this armpit of the galaxy had procedures. "Why wasn't this in my briefing?"

Henni averted his gaze, his features sunk in a worried frown.

"Your jobs are safe with me, Henni." For the time being. "What's happening at the station?"

Both of Henni's tongues ran along his lips. "The unions are saying the new talks won't help them. They fear governments will dump their unwanted people on the station to work in the dirtiest of industries, driving down wages."

"Who is Sauer speaking with now?" she asked.

Emerlynne's chest tightened. Too many unknowns. She'd inform command to postpone the talks or relocate them. Her hand reached for her wrist computer, but Henni reached out. A flare of surprise shot through Emerlynne. No one touched a Diplomatic Watch officer. No one. Ever. Not even to be pulled from a burning building.

"Sergeant Major." Henni's face returned to its normal shade of royal blue. His hands fell to his sides in dejection. "Please. No harm was meant."

Her fingers lingered over the control pad, a decision on whether to commandeer Sauer's office not yet made. "Where's Sauer?"

"He's being held hostage."

"By?"

"The unions. You can't tell anyone." Light-blue crept up his neck—fear. "He'll die if word gets out. And we'll have riots on our hands."

"How long ago?"

"Two days ago."

Two full days and her unit hadn't been appraised. What kind of amateurs were running this place? "You had seventy-hours to alert me, and no word was sent?"

"We were afraid the communications were monitored."

"How many others know?"

"Only the core administrative staff."

She jerked her thumb to three junior officers, a silent question as to what they knew.

"They're core staff." The burden in his voice eased.

"Send me all your files. Every briefing on the strikes. Every leader and organiser of the unions. Every layout, cubby hole, smuggling area, smuggler, everything you have on this station."

Henni swiped the tablet in a flurry of artistic strokes, and seconds later, her wrist-computer pinged with the receipt of a data dump.

"If anything changes, you notify me right away." She stared at him until he nodded.

With that, she took the shuttle back to the docking bay that berthed the Jubilee. The feeling of weightlessness only added to her burdens, now adrift in a mission that faced tenfold complications.

At the docking bay, people parted to allow her — no, her uniform — to pass. Movement from the corner of her eye. One of the same smugglers she'd seen before. The platinum blond man had to have diamond-hard plums to make another contact so soon after being spotted.

"Stop." Her voice boomed like a barrage of cannons.

An interruption in the shower of sparks as the welders stopped, pushed their helmets over their faces and peered down from the rafters.

The blond man, wiry with sharp cheekbones and a firm mouth that made gods weep, broke left and shoved his way through the stevedores. The second smuggler, broader in the shoulder and with a bent nose, bolted in the opposite direction, towards a series of under-construction corridors.

Emerlynne broke into a sprint, charged up a series of crates, and launched herself at the smuggler. She tackled him, rolled on her knees and pressed her weight into him.

With a grunt, he landed face first, arms pressed under him to brace his fall. She pressed her knee into the small of his back. Reaching for his arm, she whacked handcuffs on him.

"What are you doing?" He bucked against her.

"Arresting you."

"For what?"

She searched his pockets and dug out a keycard pass to the administrative pylon. "What are you doing with this?" She waved the pass in his face.

"None of your damned business."

"What are you doing with this?" She pressed her knee deeper into the hollow of his back.

He tugged on his wrists, but the handcuffs held firm. Every sinew in his neck stretched and flexed from his resistance. This man wasn't a two-bit druggy, he was street-hardened and cornered. A lethal combination.

She kneeled harder to push herself up and was rewarded with a crack of his lower back. Standing, she reached for his cuffed hands and hauled him up.

"Like it rough, do you?" A wicked smirk crossed his scarred lips.

"Move." She shoved him between his shoulders and frog-marched him to the gangway of the Jubilee.

Days' worth of grime sullied his hair. An odour lingered around him, one of grittiness and roughness.

"Name?"

"Sit on an arc welder." He spoke the words over his shoulder to the dockworkers, eliciting a round of laughter. "Remember, you saw it here. It's the point where a man can't carry out his business without the boot threads of the law on his neck."

A round of grumbles rose from the crowd. Emerlynne fought a flinch. Glacial sweat eased down her spine. One officer against dozens of workers armed with twenty-kilo wrenches and hooks with enough places to shove her into the vacuum of space. By the time her team arrived, she'd be adrift in the nebula.

Control. Order. The uniform. Her against dozens of workers who would rather her neck stretch from the rafters.

"This is a lawful arrest." Her voice held the strength of bulkheads. "He was caught smuggling drugs."

She shoved him up the gangway to the Jubilee, ignoring the workers' insults.

"Prepare an interrogation room," she said over her computer to the communications officer.

"Aye, ma'am," the comms officer replied.

A right, an elevator to three decks below, two left turns, and she pushed the perp into a holding cell flanked by two security officers. The austere cell had a bed with a thin mattress and a toilet.

Faced away from her, the suspect stood, waiting for his cuffs to be removed. The key to the irons remained in her pocket.

"What's your name?" Her voice held enough steel to repair the station.

He made a rude gesture.

"Give me the kit," she said.

A guard handed her a medical device. She plucked out more of his hairs than were needed and placed a follicle into the receptacle.

"Scanners didn't pick up weapons," a guard said.

The suspect was unarmed like the station wasn't a heap of junk in space.

Her hands reached for his shoulders, patting their wiry strength. His clothes were dirty, but not old. No fuzz or frayed seams. She ran her hands down the lengths of his arms — strong from work, not hours whiled away on exercise equipment designed for galactic corporation executives taking their pleasure yachts from one mansion to another. She patted the length of his body, following his shoulders to his tapered waist. A blaster in the small of his back, one dagger per boot, and a garrote coiled in the heel of his boot. She ran the back of her hands to the apex of his thighs.

"A little higher, and more pressure at the front," the

suspect said.

"Shut up."

"I can fill you, Peach."

Heat flared in her. She ignored him and shoved the suspect fully into the cell. Once inside, she slammed the cage shut.

The suspect flopped onto the bed. There was a gleam in his eyes that stretched a galaxy beyond cockiness.

The DNA recorder beeped, and the guard handed it back to her. She glanced at the results: no complete matches found. A partial match was found but no further information was available.

That couldn't be right. The Corps had access to all databases throughout the empire. She swiped her fingers over the DNA markers and computer banks the program had checked and she verified the connection to the station's computers. All was as it should be.

She glanced up at the suspect, the same smug expression now entrenched. He had his secrets, and she had her tricks. A few more key commands, her Cosmic-level security access, and a few new algorithms to bypass whatever encryption was on his file... and... prickles raced along her skin.

The fabric of a guard's uniform rustled when he shifted his weight.

The overhead lights hummed.

Someone walked past in the hallway, their boots squeaking against the floor.

One foot resting against the edge of the bed, the prisoner leaned his back against the wall. He stared at her as if he were a professor of celestial physics and she a dust mite.

How many words for idiot existed in the universe? Because she was every single one of them. "Why didn't you say anything?" She released the cage's lock.

"When? When I was making a buy? After you tackled me and drew the attention of hundreds of people?" Station Constable Dallin Iliev asked.

She uncuffed him. "You could have said something on the gangway. Or in the cell."

"And blow my cover? The cover that took me a year to build?" He rubbed his wrists and rolled his shoulders forward and back. "Were you a left tackle at the academy?"

She suppressed a smile and looked at her wrist-computer. The trade delegates couldn't land if the Chief Administrator was still hostage. "What happened with Sauer?"

"That's what I'm working to find out."

"You said you were undercover for one year." She flicked through his file, but there was no mention of his original mission.

"A smuggling ring's been operating on the station. We tend to look the other way for narcotics, but weapons and explosives are another matter."

"Explosives?"

"Enough to turn the station into a metal asteroid

belt." Dallin touched his toes and sighed.

Her gaze followed the length of his spine down the expanse of his shoulders to the roundness of his rump. Scorching liquid pooled deep in her belly, followed by awareness of where they were, and her mission crashed into her. "Hungry?"

"Always hungry for peaches."

Tenacious. Good. "There's a mess two decks up. I need a debrief."

"Sorry, Peach. I'm on the job." He winked. "But after—" A playful smile tugged on his marked lips.

Marked from what? An accident with a fork as a child? Too many knuckles smashing his lips against his teeth? A jaded lover who caught him cheating and marred his beautiful mouth?

He stepped around her towards the brig's door. "Not every day a smuggler gets a full meal."

Emerlynne cleared her throat and straightened her tunic. The uniform. The mission. She motioned for the guards to stay behind and escorted Dallin to the mess.

He piled roast beef and asparagus onto his plate and poured a container of gravy over it. He selected the largest mug and filled it with black tea, adding milk and sugar.

"Chef didn't make soup today." She sat opposite him.

"I prefer stew." He unfolded the napkin across his lap and cut off one small piece in a polished move that would have him at home at the royal palace.

Were there any opportunities of fine dining in this floating rust heap? She all but pulled up a notepad on her wrist computer to take notes on table etiquette.

"I'm not an animal."

"Contrary to your tone, clothes, and odour."

A roar of a laugh escaped his mouth and bounced off the steel-plated ceilings. Other crew members stared opened-mouthed and curious, but Dallin continued to laugh until he was mugged of breath.

Laughter bubbled in her. She shot her crew with her don't-ask-stare to reign it in. Damn him.

"The ring's headed by a woman named Johansson. She normally brings in drugs, but in recent months she's been bringing in weapons. A month ago, I got wind of an explosive shipment."

"What's Johansson doing with the weapons?"

"Some go to the striking workers. Enough to fight back against station security." He cut a piece of asparagus followed by a small piece of roast beef, let the gravy drip off his fork, and ate it. "I don't know about the rest. Haven't heard any whispers about attacking the talks."

"What's the mood on the talks?" A message from the bridge flashed on her wrist-computer. She ordered the captain to remain docked at the station, uppity dock workers be damned.

Dallin walked to the cafeteria counter, helped himself to more roast beef, asparagus, piled sweet potatoes, and returned. "Life of a poor smuggler. Mostly vegetable soup, jerky, and protein bars." He lifted his gaze towards the desert section of the mess eyeing the pies. "When you get the chance to eat—"

"Every pylon on Archimedes has a different opinion on the talks. The administrative, cultural, habitat and leisure pylons are in favour of the talks, to varying degrees."

"Explain."

"The administrative and leisure pylons are eager for more funding and more people visiting. The cultural pylon is interested in the talks, but not if it ruins the economic prospects of the artists born on the station. They don't want other artist colonies setting up here, stealing ideas and ruining the brand." Dallin rose to collect a piece of pecan pie with two servings of vanilla ice cream.

"Don't they pay you?"

A lop-sided grin tugged on his features, drawing out the dimple in his left cheek. "We've been over this, Peach. I have to look the part. Real smugglers are lean and built for a fight. Besides, good, free food is hard to come by."

She glanced down at his service record on her wrist computer. From the hollows on his cheeks and the sinewy tissue of his forearms, he'd lost thirty kilos since the photo was taken. All wiry lines, instead of fleshed-out bits with full cheeks and thicker arms.

Shame, that.

"And the weapons that aren't going to the workers?" she asked.

"That's what I'm following. Some guns are going to the industry pylon. Some are being transshipped to other parts of the galaxy, most to insurrections and wars I've never heard of. But there's a small portion that's being kept on the station."

"For criminals?"

He ate his first piece of pecan pie, and eyelids eased closed. A low, seductive 'hmm' rumbled up his throat. Dallin, the undercover police officer of over a year with hollowed-out features, disappeared, and the real Dallin appeared. The one who had a sweet tooth and a healthy appetite, the one whose roots weren't platinum blond but a darker shade of brown.

"I'm not sure where they're going." And with that, Dallin the undercover cop re-emerged.

"What about agitation? Instigators looking to change the politics of Archimedes. Separate from the Empire?"

"Separate? This station leaves the empire, and two things happen. First, they lose all subsidies to keep the lights on, health care and education. Second, every fleet within ten parsecs descends on the station to take control over it. Leave it here or tow it away, whichever way that power wants to seize it." He eyed the dessert section again but remained seated.

He couldn't still be hungry. "It's a space heap."

He snorted and made a forceful swallow of his strawberry shortcake tart. The blueness of his eyes put the azure of the royal crest to shame.

"It's worth more than it looks." Gone was the two-bit smuggler. In his place was a cop delivering a strategic analysis. "It's moveable to any hot spot in the sector. Laser cannons can be mounted on the pylons. Torpedo bays can be retrofitted. In the wrong hands, this can be a planet-killer. It's millions of tonnes of steel that can be resold. It's a cheap pool of labour to make spaceships."

"Where does that leave us?" Us. A word she wished she could reel back into her mouth.

"Soon, Peach. After the mission." The playfulness in his tone did nothing to soothe the crackle of her nerves.

She was a Sergeant Major of the Diplomatic Corps. Peach? Should she call him plum? Plums? She smiled inwardly. Plums. The mission. The weapons. The explosives. The diplomatic delegation that I'm sworn to protect.

"All mission, no play?"

"It's the uniform. The code." The years of instruction drilled into her since birth of the importance of maintaining family honour. The hours she spent with aching muscles training in hand-to-hand combat. The endless minutes where she was forced to stand in the rain, wrestle fellow students in knee-deep mud, and run the length of an obstacle course to build her strength and endurance.

"Nothing else but the uniform?" he asked.

Beyond his seductive smile, his table manners he'd acquired, somehow, and the way he scanned the room, edgy, despite being around friendlies.

"Yes," she said.

"I need a way off of this ship. Something plausible, something that allows me to keep my cover."

"I'm going with you."

He rocked his head back as if she'd told him the sun imploded. "I assure you, one-year deep cover, I can survive."

"The lives of the delegates are my responsibility. We do this together. I need details. A way to reach out. A way to bail you out in case something happens."

He leaned down into the top of his boot, retrieved a small patch of film, and handed it to her.

Where did that come from? She'd searched him herself.

He shot her a he-has-his-tricks-she-has-her-secrets look. "I'm going to check on an informant. He'll know what Johansson's up to."

"Which informant?" She smoothed the flimsy fibre over the back of her hand. The material dissolved into her skin, and seconds later, her wrist computer flashed with new information.

"I need a reason to get back out there," he said.

She let his non-answer slide. Cops and their informants. Priests and their confessors. "Not enough evidence?"

"Of smuggling when you found me with a stolen keycard?" He shot her a get-real stare.

"Give me a story."

"Make my face pretty." He drank the rest of his tea, rose from his stool, and braced himself.

Dallin's jaw ached with a throb that spanned a light-year. He needed rum, a dentist, and an icepack. Instead, he got one hell of a left hook to the chin, an ass-kicking down the gangway, and a gush of blood from a busted lip.

Hands cuffed behind his back, he stumbled to the loading bay and came to a crashing halt against a stack of crates.

Click. The handcuffs released.

Ping. His steel bracelets fell against the dock.

He spat blood on the floor.

Defiant, Peach stood with her hands hanging by her sides at the top of the gangway ready to take every worker single handedly. She pinned him with a try-me stare, a dare to Dallin and everyone else who would challenge the law. No—a dare to challenge her.

Where was she ten years ago, before the ex-wife, before his heart turned to stone, before his job became everything, leaving him hollow and hardened?

"That's right. You did your best and failed." He rolled his stiff shoulders, stretched his sore neck side to side, and strode past the gathering throng to an access corridor.

Brushing past damaged overhead wires, he pressed

into the corridor. Hundreds of metres away from the dock, he slid a metal grate away from the wall, stepped into it, then slid moved the grate back.

Metal screeched against metal. Seconds later, darkness enclosed him.

"You're alone," Peach said in his earpiece. Did her voice become sultrier since leaving the ship? Or was it because she whispered in his ear, low words meant only for him?

"Not when you're with me, Peach." Adjusting his contact lenses to the darkness, he strode along the access way until he reached an unfinished cargo bay that was supposed to have been completed years ago. Budget cuts, strikes, and lack of commerce combined into a mess that left many passageways and large spaces ignored.

Perfect for criminals, a nightmare for law enforcement.

"What intel do you need? I'm patched in." The smoothness of her words tugged at his ear, drawing him closer.

"Check for heat signatures in these passages." Something small and fast scurried by. From behind him, dozens of small claws grated against metal.

"There are four people ahead in the tunnels to the north."

"Don't worry about them."

"Why?"

"It's a drug den." Hand trailing along the wall, his fingers skimmed various indentations left behind by different criminals. Each left their markings to indicate which passage to take back to this docking bay or that. He adjusted his contact lenses for low lighting and ignored a mischief of rats scuttling around the edges of the walls.

He muted the comms and pressed forward into the darkness, breaking out into a jog when he was clear of the drug den. A throb started from the tip of his chin and pulsed up his jaw. Why'd the woman hit so hard? Because a woman like that never pulled punches. Ever.

After two kilometres of half-finished tunnels, his feet eased off the floor. He sucked in a last complete lungful he'd have for the next five klicks. Near weightless, his toes dragged against the floor. He pushed off the ground and propelled himself into the darkness.

One good thing about this section of tunnels—the rats stayed away. Turns out rats weren't fond of floating. Good, because he wasn't enthused about bumping into them and them scratching and biting his face.

A lesson learned the hard way. One he'd never need to relearn.

He continued his trajectory towards the industrial pylon. The pressures of space popped his ears. Another fifteen minutes, and he'd be at the base of the pylon. Two minutes after that, his ears would pop again.

Cold seeped into his bones, robbing his fingers of feeling. His lips numbed, and the air thinned. Breathable atmosphere, but only just. Toes dragging against the floor, he settled his weight back down and gave his body a minute to regain its senses.

Ignoring the prickles of cold against his lungs, he jogged out of the incomplete tunnels and stepped into the robotics manufacturing compound. Reverberations pinged off the industrial metal corridors, a steady rhythm of yells and stomps. Eyes adjusting to brightness, he switched his contact lenses back to normal lighting. He stood behind a series of crates, listening to a raucous crowd shout insults and slogans. Body acclimated, he stepped out to the edge of the mob.

The same angry faces as those of the dockworkers, only with different features and uniforms. Different slogans spewed at the same cadence. Poverty and rage mixed in a roar.

A cluster of workers, some Ulian with enraged dark blue faces and Vissini's with their feathered crests raised in indignation, shook their fists at the people overhead. On the gangway directly over the work area, senior management in formal attire glowered at the masses.

Dallin lingered at the edges of the crowd. Shouts of 'higher wages,' 'good work,' 'better living conditions,' and 'fairness' swirled around the workers.

The mouths of management moved, but their voices drowned in a sea of chants. Good thing Dallin read lips; unfortunately, the lips in question read 'never in a million years,' 'stupid demands,' 'die.'

A worker hurled a wrench towards the grated walkway where management stood scowling at the masses. A second. And a third. A reverse-rain of metal and tools pelted the executives on the metallic passage. All but the owner of the robotics plants stood, defiant, shouting obscenities. The rest fled for the aisles. Until one tool hit the owner on the head, drawing blood.

Physics demonstrated its nasty habit of being a universal constant. All the wrenches and tools fell down in a brutal hail of metal and pain. The workers scattered like a school of fish changing directions on a pinpoint. Strikers fled to the corners of the factory, ducking out of the way of twenty-kilo metal rain drops. A few unlucky labourers collapsed to the ground, the tops of their heads bashed in from falling tools.

A round of gasps from the workers, followed by a chorus of yells. A few bold people ventured forward to tend the wounded and dead, but most continued their fierce chants.

Petty snitch Caleb Forrest scampered away to the shadows and nooks that were his home.

Dallin crossed the assembly line, through the crowd of protesters. A crush of workers in orange and yellow uniforms clamoured up metal stairs towards the over-head walkway.

In the press, Dallin lost sight of his informant and was shoved against the wall. A fist drove into his abdomen, followed by another. Dallin raised his hands to defend himself, but had his legs swept out from under him. A flurry of stomps against his chest caused something inside of him to snap.

A siren blew, one loud enough to start another

universe. The lighting in the room shifted from bright to blue; the Station Constabulary was intervening.

Bitter shouts turned to angry ones. The workers rushed forward to the police until they met with force in the middle, turning into a melee of knuckles and wrenches against trudgens and shields. Screams. Clashes. Cracks. Metal tools clattered against the floor.

Laser blasts electrified the air filling it with sweat, blood, and singed skin.

"What the hell were you thinking?" Peach looped an arm around Dallin's waist and pulled him away from the fracas. A series of stern-faced, clean-cut, polished-boot members of Peach's team, fell in around them.

Her team.

The riot's clatter echoed in the hallway. A handful of workers stumbled out of the manufacturing floor and scampered up the corridor, leaving behind a trail of blood.

Heavy thumps clanged against the wall as body and after body slammed against it. Who was winning? Dallin couldn't tell.

"What are you doing here?" He pulled himself taller, though not entirely straight, the pain in his kidney still stabbing.

"Saving your ass." Peach's words were even, commanding.

Never had he wanted a woman so much in his life.

"I was holding my own," he said.

"You were getting the shit kicked out you." She

looped her hand around his waist and helped him up the hallway. "Why are you grinning? I didn't hit your head that hard." Her hands pressed into him.

He wanted all of him pressed into all of her. "I found a way to ease the pain." He ignored the stinging cascade that rocked his body. "Why are you here?"

"You went silent. That wasn't part of the deal. Where were you heading?"

"How'd you find me?" he asked.

"You have your ways. I have mine."

Just when he thought he'd caught his breath; there she was to steal it again. He rubbed his cheek, where she had slapped him on the Jubilee before kicking him off her ship. "You put a patch on me." Like the one he had given her for her hand.

Branded.

Rioters poured from the hallways. Individual slogans blended into a racket of anger and frustration. The metal plates under his feet trembled. Her team formed a box around them, hands-on their blasters, poised to draw.

"Who were you going to speak with?" she asked.

"My informant."

"Who?" She activated her wrist computer.

"Caleb Forrest."

"A two-bit snitch?"

"Forrest knows more what's going on in the station than your best intelligence officer." Dallin led her away from the riot, down a series of corridors leading to the main thoroughfare, fish swimming upstream against a torrent of Station Constabulary officers in full riot gear. A burst of recognition flashed across two of the officers' faces — old card buddies — from a time when Dallin wasn't undercover and had friends.

Was there really ever such a time? Eons ago, maybe.

New blood drawn, fresh bruises welted, a second tooth in need of dental attention, Dallin led them to the far end of the industrial area towards a series of hole-in-the-wall bars, where Forrest would be. Where Forrest always was, eavesdropping for his next secret, reaching into his next mark's pocket, lurking for opportunities to pounce.

Away from the fray, Dallin eased his pace. The stitch in his side a combination of too much food, adrenaline, and a shit-kicking. "I can't go in there with a swat team."

"They're not a swat team."

He cocked his head towards the escorts. Despite their work clothes, they were all immaculate. Each with never-used knee pads and buzzcuts and neatly pulled-back hair in buns reserved for cafeteria workers, correctional wardens, and ballerinas. That, and cops.

A slight change in her eyes, a recognition of how well her team didn't blend in. "Keep a perimeter of thirty metres."

With crisp steps, her team fanned out, keeping to the corridor's edges and main industrial entrance. They became a sea of shapes draped in white linen against a canvas of grease, robotic assembly lines, and metal. A non-camouflaged fit.

"Where are you going, Peach?"

"With you."

How far would she go? With him. More than an hour, but less than a lifetime? Forever? "Forrest's skittish. If he sees you, he'll bolt."

"Why?"

"He's used to seeing me alone."

"Make up some story. That I'm your long-lost sister."

With how his thoughts wandered every time he looked at her, they couldn't be siblings. "It won't work."

"I'm some action you've been keeping on the side." She unpinned her hair. Cascades of midnight locks fell to her mid-back. She threaded her fingers to loosen the strands and unbuttoned the top two buttons of her blouse revealing a kissable and nibble-able swathe of creamy skin.

He stumbled first on his tongue then over his feet, and she caught him. Her delicious scent of honey and fruit curled around him, and it was all he could do to not press his bruised lips against her soft mouth.

"Do you need medical attention?" She cupped his face and peered into his eyes. She tracked one finger across his field of vision for him to follow.

He needed attention. Her attention. Only her attention. Until he fell into a coma from sexual exhaustion — a term he'd coin from his activities with her. "I'll take getting roughed up by you any day."

"Is that a bet?"

He stifled a groan, his hands burning to rest on the curve of her hips. This mission couldn't be over fast enough. It'd be her, him, and some corner of the station where the gravity plates didn't work. "You're my girl-friend. Stay behind me."

"If I'm your girlfriend, I'm in front of you to keep you from getting killed." She stepped into the bar before him, the flashing neon yellow lights drawing out the determination in her eyes.

Damn woman. Damn infuriating woman who'd ensure he'd never sleep for the rest of his life.

"What does he look like?" Peach strode towards the bar, motioned for two drinks to the bartender, and turned to face the dingy joint.

"Like every other informant. Skittish. Opportu-nistic. Greedy."

"That guy over there?" She lifted her chin in a subtle movement towards the far corner, the one with the poorest lighting.

Forrest, with his shifty eyes and high-strung demea-nour, sat on the edge of his seat. The bulk of his weight ready to club and smash his way to the nearest exits.

"I'll take a run at him." Peach downed her whiskey in one gulp. She moved away from the bar, leaving him with the bill.

His cracked smile pained his cheeks. He held his wrist out for the bartender to reconcile payment. Dallin pushed forward and surpassed Peach on her indirect approach to Forrest.

Forrest's gaze followed Peach, her every sensuous movement, the way she rocked her head back and laughed when she stopped to chat with a cluster of workers. Her hand lingered on the arm of a labourer. A love-struck grin crossed Forrest's face.

Shit. Did Dallin have that same idiotic smile on his? Not possible. Not with his bruised cheeks and busted lips. It would hurt too much.

She broke away from the knot of wrench-heads, gliding her way towards Forrest.

A left tackle, a ballerina, and an actress. What other hidden talents did Peach have? Ankles behind ears? Memorised the encyclopedia? The only person in the galaxy that consumed his thoughts. No. Her real talent rested in having the strength to challenge him, put him in his place, and surpass him.

Dallin flopped on the bench next to Forrest and draped an arm over his shoulder. "What's happening?"

Forrest startled and pushed against Dallin's shoulder. Dallin pulled Forrest tighter against him. In another time and place, the position might be mistaken for two long-lost university friends reunited. But this was not that time, nor that place and Dallin pushed Forrest to the bench. Peach settled on the opposite side of Forrest, a sweet smile on her lips that did nothing to mask the intensity of her eyes.

"What's going on?" Dallin swept his gaze across

the crowded bar. He could have walked in naked with fireworks exploding on his head, handing five hundred credits to each person and no one would have noticed. All eyes were on Peach.

"What do you mean?" Forrest's voice sputtered like a dying engine.

Peach elbowed him.

Forrest winced. "There's something wrong at the docks."

Horrendous music blared on the speakers. Some horrible twanging of instruments that passed as culture for the dockworkers on the station. Patrons hunched over their drinks and continued to send longing glances towards Peach.

"Explain," Dallin said.

"Workers are receiving weapons. High-grade weapons."

"From?"

"Hell, if I know, but they're expensive."

"How are they paying for them?"

Forest shrugged. "A credit here, a credit there, pool them, and you've got enough." He downed his drink and rose to leave, but Peach grabbed him by the belt and yanked him back down to the bench.

His woman. Or perhaps he was Peach's man. The second one sounded better.

Forest landed with a thump and a yelp. "I told you all that I know."

"Who's bringing in the explosives?" Peach asked.

"The unions." The snitch wrestled his shirt away from Peach's grip.

"Who's got the Chief Administrator? Sauer?" Dallin and Peach asked in unison.

"The unions," Forest said.

"Why?" Dallin asked.

"Easier to control the station that way. Detain the administrator, and work comes to a halt."

Detain the Chief Administrator, distract law enforcement with the strikes, attack the diplomats. Clean. Simple. Deadly.

"Work's still ongoing, docks are still under repair," Dallin said. "Replacement parts for ships are being made."

"That's not the real work."

"What do you mean?" Dallin asked.

"The real work's in the channels, the tunnels, the coming and going of ships. Notice a drop in ships docking?" Forest shoved his way past Dallin and seconds later, Forest slipped out of the bar.

Peach made to stand, but Dallin reached for her hand. "Let him go."

Skin on skin. His nerve endings electrified. Peach glanced over at him, a decision played on her face, before she lowered herself to sit beside him. Their arms touched. The heat of her body brought out a different throb in him, one that sent blood rushing to every part of him but his brain.

"Think the unions have Sauer?" Peach asked.

"It's possible."

"Need solid intelligence."

"The unions have been butting heads with Sauer for years. They went the extra step? Bought explosives. Kidnapped him."

"Who's Johansson?" Peach asked. "What of her involvement?"

"Runs the largest gambling racket. Don't have proof yet of her involvement."

"Where is she? I need to interrogate her."

"She keeps her office at a gaming hole not far from here. We'll go there." Before he finished his sentence, Peach was on her feet, heading towards the exit.

He caught up with her, and they picked their way through the corridor. The clamour from the riots still ringing off metal hallways. Police reinforcements descended on the place, shoving passersby against the walls. A cop kitted out with a shield and trudgen advanced on Peach. She squared her chin, the way prizefighters and drill sergeants and generals did when asserting their dominance. Recognition shimmered in the officer's eyes—she was of them—and he changed course.

Cops. They all looked, acted, and smelled the same except Peach. She had a presence to command an army, the mind of a chess master, and the ass of a goddess. They made their way up the hallway, lost in the flow of people fleeing the riots. Something close by burned. Overhead lights changed from yellow to blue, and an authoritative voice came over the station intercom, demanding people return to their quarters.

No one listened. Only a crush of people heading out towards the bars, gaming hells, and commons areas.

"Here." Dallin placed his hand on Peach's lower back and guided her to an establishment in a side corridor. She leaned into his hand, enough for his fingers to trace over the sensuous curve of her lower back. She shifted her weight and his hand slipped to the swell of her hip.

"Like that." She bumped her hip against his hand, a perfect fit.

He developed tunnel vision on the seductive curve of her cheeks.

Two bartenders eyed them warily. A live jazz band played in the corner, their music a steady beat to the chaos outside. Dozens of degenerates flopped chips on tables, called for cards, threw dice, and spun wheels.

"She'll be at the back." He leaned closed to her, his lips brushing against her ear.

She softened against him. More of her. Less of the music, stale beer, and plot to blow something up.

Drunks sat at the bar, staring into the abyss of their drinks. Bartenders prepared orders and signalled servers to pick them up. Heavy-set guards in expensive suits and jaws straighter than plumb lines, moved to intercept Dallin and Peach.

Dallin pounded his fist against a metallic door to the right of the bar, the last unbruised bone in his body — his pinky — joined the others in pain. When no response came, Peach raised her polished boot and stomped on the handle. Three stomps later, the hinges loosened. Dallin launched into the door, stumbling into the narrow corridor towards Johannsson's office.

Something large and heavy hurled past him, landing hard against the wall. Laying on the floor, one of Johansson's guards blinked with unfocused eyes.

A second body crashed to the floor. Peach whirled around, grabbed a third guard in a wristlock, and manoeuvred the burly man to the ground. "Where's Johansson?"

"Over there." The guard raised a trembling finger down the hallway. She cranked his wrist to an unnatural angle, something cracked, and she let it fall.

A small room at the end of the hallway led to a private gaming chamber. High stakes. Hundreds of thousands of credits. Spaceships. Equity in an industrial or dock concern in the station. A private continent on a tropical planet. A floating mansion over the ridges of Alemn. Things that mattered.

Johansson sat at the far end of the table, three towers of credits in front of her, each reaching her chin. Her cold eyes calculated odds. Thin in the cheek to the point of emaciation, she looked five hundred calories away from death.

She flopped her cards on the table — straight flush. One woman with the jowls of a basset hound stared in disbelief as Johansson raked in the credits.

A player made a straggling noise and clutched his chest. His face turned darker purple than his expensive jacket. Sweat beaded in his temple and he hinged forward, gaze still locked on his losing hand.

Heart attack.

Two of Johansson's guards stepped in and hooked arms under the player's shoulders, pulling him away from the table.

"You're the one who dealt." Johansson made a show of tugging her non-existent cuffs. "It's not like I can hide anything in my short-sleeved shirt."

"Need a word," Dallin said.

"I'm busy." In another life, with more food in her, Johansson could have graced the cover of every magazine in the galaxy. But this was not that life.

"If you want a chance to use the proceeds you've earned, you'll speak with him." Peach moved to stand next to Johansson.

"New toy?" Johansson tilted her head towards Peach.

Playmate. Partner. Perfection.

He ignored Johansson's comment. "What have you heard of Sauer?" There. Direct. No sense in dancing around a subject when the Archimedes was a tinderbox and someone was running around with high explosives.

"I play cards." Johansson shuffled the deck and cut the deck. "Sometimes, I play with others." Her eyes flashed something mischievous and she cocked her head towards Peach. "But she gives me the impression she doesn't want to share."

He didn't share. Ever. And most certainly not Peach.

Johansson dealt a hand, her expression as blank as an unused sheet of paper. Her gaze swept her opponent's faces, a moment passed, and she placed her bet.

Peach slammed her fist on the table. Credits and chips danced.

"Didn't anyone tell you not to splash the pot?" Johansson shook her head. "It's bad form."

"Lives are at risk," Peach said.

"Not mine."

"How much you want to bet?"

Dallin's lips twisted in an unbridled smile. Ten years of exile might be worth it, after all.

Emerlynne glowered at Johansson. If any diplomat was injured during their talks, the sector would be at war. If Chief Administrator Sauer wasn't found by the end of the day, she'd have the talks relocated. If the explosives weren't discovered within an hour, she'd send her team back to the Jubilee and tell them to wait ten thousand kilometres away until they received word from her.

Except they were her team. And they wouldn't leave her behind. Nor would they leave explosives behind or Sauer hostage. She would do the same. Finish the mission, even when mission parameters changed. Even when there was mission creep and it wasn't clear what needed to be done: seize explosives, release a hostage, negotiate a labour dispute, quell riots, secure the location, or get the hell out of here.

And there was Dallin. Why did he have that foolish grin on his face, somewhere between a daydream and wet dream? The intensity in his eyes ignited something inside her.

"Chief Administrator Sauer, who has him?" Emerlynne used her cut-the-crap tone.

"Some union's got him."

"Why?"

"Talk. Laws. Rules." Johansson folded her hand. "Who cares so long as people keep giving me their money."

"What have you heard?" Dallin asked.

"The nebula's nice to see this time of day. Take shuttle six for the best view."

Something ticked inside Emerlynne. She swiped the pot away and leaned both hands on the table. "Has anyone smuggled anything unusual to the station?"

The players gasped and reached greedy fingers for the chips. Johansson's guards moved to intercept, but Dallin stood watch. Lean, mean, and ready to brawl.

"Drugs. People. Booze." Johansson restacked her chips.

Welts and bruises masked Dallin's expression, but his eyes erupted in anger. "I'm calling in a chit."

A crease, followed by a second, until an accordion of creases marred Johannson's brow. "You sure you want to waste a favour from me?"

"You heard me." He lifted his battered chin towards Johansson's bodyguards. "They heard me."

A bold move. The right move. She'd thank him later for it. A dozen ways came to mind. None involved thank-you cards, gift cards, or baskets of muffins. All involved, pecan pie with whipped cream and vanilla ice cream, booze, and sex.

"What has she done to you?" Johansson asked, a slender woman at a table of heavy weights, every word from her a knockout. "Who uses explosives?"

A forty-pound wrench dropped from the second storey.

Boom.

The crux of the matter.

"Industrial applications," Emerlynne said, "but they wouldn't have to smuggle it in. There are licenses and channels for that."

"And?" Johansson placed a bet.

"A terrorist attack," Dallin said. "Strap some bombs to a pylon or a ship, wait for trade delegates to arrive."

"Is he always this predictable? Kiss, suck, lick, finish? Or does he change things up with suck, kiss, lick, and finish?" Johansson asked.

Embattled and emboldened, Dallin stood his ground. A knock-down, drag-'em-out fighter to the last.

"The man can blush. Well, under the bruises. Never

pegged you for someone who likes it rough." Johansson placed a bet. "But can he think? You get one last chance. Who buys explosives and why?"

Bruised and battered, Dallin squared his shoulders, ready for the next round, the last round. A thousand silent words exchanged between them.

Industry. Terrorists. Hijackers. Who else would have use for explosives? Construction crews. Military. Mining companies.

"Celebrations," Dallin said.

Every muscle in her body puckered. This was it. Her mission's failure. The death of thousands of innocent people. A sector on the brink of war.

Johansson dealt a round of cards, stared at her opponents and placed a bet without looking at her hand. "I do believe we have a winner."

A winner? Dallin was right? Of course, he was right. One year in the metal trenches of his place, he'd have smarts and instincts and wiry frame forged from fight. She could kiss his swollen lips. "Who's celebrating what?"

"Ha!" One of the Ulian women card players wrapped her arms around the pot. The corner of one tongue stuck out the corner of her mouth, and the other licked her lower lip.

"I don't work for you, and you're costing me money." Johansson made a dismissive motion with her hand.

Dallin stepped beside Emerlynne, his hand finding

the exact spot on the curve of her hip she had instructed him to touch.

Quick study.

"We need to leave," he said.

To somewhere private with a soft bed. Or a table. Or a sofa. Either would do. She slid her gaze to the far wall, a move to quell her sensuous thoughts. The mission. The trade delegates. The bombs.

The heat that pooled lower in her belly.

Outside of the bar, her team arrested a score of rioters. Some with a few new bruises, some with a trickle of blood down their noses, all with defeat stamped on their faces.

Good. Balance was restored.

"Celebrations? What was that about?" Emerlynne followed Dallin to an elevator.

"Who buys fireworks?"

"Fireworks?" The pieces slowly rearranged in Emerlynne's mind. "You think the people behind the plot to kidnap Sauer used the talk's celebrations to smuggle in explosives?"

"It's a possibility." Dallin pressed the button. "Look up who was in charge of the celebrations."

She swiped her wrist computer. "It seems Henni was in charge of it."

"Who?"

She pulled up the photo of the administrative worker who had told them Sauer had been kidnapped.

"He's part of the working classes, and he wants a

raise, only their union isn't good enough to call for strike action? He and a few friends smuggle in explosives?"

Henni wasn't a rebellious kind. Too wrapped up in appearances and protocol. "Why go to that effort? He's got access to Administration files. He could steal secrets, change budgets, blackmail."

"Something's not right." He speared his hair.

"How do you want to play this?"

A mischievous smile tugged his lips. "I only play one way. Slow."

She ignored his comment, but something deep inside of her yelled yes. "He's a junior administrator. He's used to being told what to do. Approach him like a friend."

Dallin held the shuttle door open for her and they travelled to the administration pylon. The brightness of the reception area blinded her. All whitewash and polish compared to grease and shadows of the industrial pylon.

"Any news?" With the grace of a panther, Henni swaggered towards them. "We've heard of riots in the industrial area and—"

"We know what happened," Emerlynne said. "I get it."

"Pardon?" Henni asked.

"I get that you're tired of working for low pay and being ignored."

"I don't understand."

"It's hard doing this job," Emerlynne said. "Long

hours. Crappy pay. People looking down at you all the time."

"What is this about, Sergeant Major?" Henni shook his head.

"The explosives." Dallin's tone was pass-the-salt casual. "What did you do with them?"

"The explosives?" Henni asked.

"The ones you were in charge of for the celebrations," Dallin said.

"I ordered them to commemorate the talks, as I was instructed to do." Henni stammered. He swiped his tablet and pulled up requisition orders. "See. Sauer gave the order, I placed it and it was received a week ago."

"By whom?" Emerlynne asked.

"By Asteroid Supplies."

"Why send fireworks to them?" Emerlynne frowned.

"They have secure storage facilities."

It couldn't be the administrative staff nor the miners. A string of curses flew from Dallin's mouth, causing his tendons to jump from his neck.

Emerlynne communicated with her team to secure the Asteroid Supplies storage facilities and wait until she arrived. She overrode the shuttle's commands, ensuring they arrived in record time.

They rounded the corner of the hallway.

"Sergeant Major?" Winters stood at the entrance, hand on his blaster, body poised to fight. "The door's locked."

"Sauer will be in there." She swiped her wrist computer, pulled up the warehouse's schematics, and performed an infrared scan. "Three people are in there." Standing in a small cluster.

Dallin turned his back to her team and leaned into her. His stubbled cheek ran against hers, sending a tingle of desire though her. A sensation of his pebbled jaw on her breast rocked her.

"No one's tied down," he said.

"Are you sure Sauer's in there? It's a large station." She groped for another question, another sentence fragment, anything to keep Dallin inches from her face. Anything to have his lips on hers.

"Let's find out." Dallin reached into his boot, took out his blaster, and readied for the incursion.

Using Cosmic-level access codes, she released the door, and reached for her weapon. She stormed in shoulder-to-shoulder with Dallin and Winters as backup.

"Diplomatic Watch. You're under arrest." She and Dallin pressed forward into the chamber, her team fanned out, one third to the right, one third to the left, and the other third sweeping behind her. A giant peacock plume of Corp officers clad in white adorned by metal and energy cartridges.

Two of the three men in the cargo bay reached for their weapons and fired. The third man bolted for a stack of containers.

Emerlynne fired, her shot landing squarely in

the chest of a shooter. He didn't go down. Instead, he reloaded his weapon and continued to discharge.

Dallin pulled her to a stack of crates and placed his hand on her head, pushing her below the tallest crate. "What the hell were you thinking?"

"Making an arrest."

"If you're suicidal. Why didn't you seek cover when he had you in his sights?"

"We're Diplomatic Corps. We head straight in."

"No negotiations, then?" His lips twisted in a scarred smile.

She ignored him; the only way she could not laugh.

Laser blasts pinged around them.

Dallin peered around the edge of the containers and frowned. "They're armoured."

"You think?"

"That's high-grade military tech. Ikissian if I had to wager."

"Aim for the head?" She poked her head above the crate, released a shot, and ducked down. Three blasts released above them, landing against the metal casings of a container. Sparks rained, landing on her thigh and on his shoulders. She patted down his back, relishing his firmness.

"Later, Peach. When I can give you a back rub in return." He fired three shots, placing his back against the cargo container.

"On three, we overwhelm them," she spoke into her wrist and received a round of affirmatives from her team.

Blasts came from behind them. Showers of sparks exploded leaving singe marks.

Startled, she slid down the containers and peered towards the door. One dozen armed guards streamed in and encircled her team. Winters and Dale moved up, firing three shots before changing positions. Three of her team pressed down towards the cargo bay door, letting loose another salvo. They continued this rapid-burst, move, rapid-bust, move pattern to disorient the criminals.

The stench of scorched metal pricked her nose. Emerlynne glanced left and right, catching sight of her team moving into better positions. She swiped her wrist computer, alerting the station police.

A formation of six guards entered the bay from the main entrance, sweeping right. An exchange of fire led to a stalemate, and the guards retreated to the hallway.

"Any tunnels leading into here?" she asked Dallin.

"All are blocked. None would lead anywhere useful."

"Where do they lead?"

"To the next cargo bay." Dallin rubbed his knee.

"You hit?"

"No." He stretched his leg out, brought it back under him, and repeated the motion several times.

"You getting old?"

The corners of his mouth pinched in a tight smile. "Never too old, Peach."

"Any way out of the next cargo bay?" She glanced at her wrist computer and pulled up the schematics. None. She knew the response before Dallin answered. She switched the view to infrared.

One man moved along the cargo bay walls next door.

"What's he doing?" Dallin peered at her wrist computer, his cheek grazing hers.

"Pacing? Trying to find a way out?"

"The door's right there." Dallin tapped the screen. "He had plenty of time to leave. Long before reinforcements arrived."

Emerlynne watched the man walk the length of the bay, up a service ladder, and along the walkway. Having finished his round, he descended the ladder, opened the cargo bay door, stepped outside and walked past a throng of guards.

Laying explosives.

Breath squeezed out of her. One cargo bay away would be ground zero. Tens of thousands of lives depended on them stopping the explosion.

"They know him," Dallin said. "Whoever that is, is their leader."

Sweat trickled the length of her spine. What was she missing? She checked the air quality of the cargo bay and swore. "Out. Everyone. Out." She lay suppressing fire.

An instant later, Dallin sprang next to her, laying down fire. A lightning storm of bolts and blasts swirled in the cargo bay. Winters and Dale lead the charge out of the bay, tackling two guards.

"Out," Emerlynne shouted about the fray. "Your boss is going to blow this up." She grabbed Dallin by the scruff of his shirt and pulled him towards the door. Something seared her thigh, but she charged forward, shooting her way past a scrambling line of guards. Two downed criminals, now a third. Her team streamed out of the bay and held the corridor, creating a pocket for her and Dallin.

Once in the hallway, she punched the control panel and the bay doors locked shut. Pain bolted up her leg, tearing across every nerve. Her lungs stretched and contracted with impossible speed. A blast of lighting scorched her hair and seared the wall before her. Something hard and hot and heavy landed squarely between her shoulders. She stumbled. Two firm hands looped around her waist and pulled her along.

Her feet pushed her forward, but her knees buckled. Her hips peddled, but her boots no longer touched by the ground. A strong arm looped around her shoulders and dragged her along, then she was weightless, a series of hands and arms wrapped around her supporting her.

Consciousness fleeting, some moments clear, many others fading. The metal floor gave way to the tiled floor of the shuttle. Jostling. So much jostling. The air grew thin and hot. Pants and gulps of air ricocheted off the glass ceiling.

"Did you stop Sauer?" she asked before passing out.

Rolling snores quaked into Emerlynne's consciousness. She'd been comfortable and asleep, now she was half-awake and in pain. Every nerve ending was stripped down to excruciation. Head propped up by a pillow, lying on her side with her arm resting on something firm, she inhaled deeply.

Plums and mechanic's oil and virility.

Dallin.

He was beside her, his warmth enveloping her.

A fragment of a memory came back to her. The cargo hold. A shard of a memory of her mission returned. Protect the diplomats. A lingering cologne of gravy.

She rolled onto her back.

Mistake.

Crippling pain gripped her spine and yanked her head back. Unable to breathe, she rolled back onto her side, where a warm hand settled on her hip.

"Easy there." Dallin's breath caressed her cheeks. "You've been shot in the back and thigh."

A shower of stars streamed across her vision. She sucked in large breaths that only sent more pain through her.

Click. Quickly followed by a second.

"I've called the nurse. He'll be here in a moment to give you something." Dallin stroked the curve of her hip. "It won't be long, Peach."

"Is everyone safe?"

"All of your crew are."

A little bit of pain relief. Wait. Her crew was fine. "What about you?" She struggled to prop herself to her elbow. Agony weighed her down. When she could open her eyes fully, she'd inspect him head to toe. For now, she ran a hand the length of his chest, feeling a bubble of fake skin.

"A few more scars to impress you, Peach." His tone was light, but his breath laboured.

"The station? The people? What happened?"

"Nothing serious."

"What of the perps?"

"Under arrest. Some are in the hospital. How'd you figure Sauer was rigging the explosives?"

"His movements. They were too methodical, as if checking on things. Wires and timers." She smacked her lips, swallowing past their dryness. "And Sauer?" She settled her head against his chest, easing an ache in her heart.

"Sauer's been caught." His thumb stroked the line of her hip. "How'd you know?"

"Sauer owns a mining company."

"And?"

"Fake his kidnapping to get attention and sympathy. Gain control over the station by intentionally failing to negotiate the end of a strike. Blow something up. Mine the rare minerals and get the contract to rebuild."

Dallin grunted.

The nurse administered something potent and blissful and left.

"Rest." He leaned forward, pressed a kiss to her lips. His slowed breath was soon followed by another round of snoring.

Eyes closing, she spread her fingers across his chest, branded by his touch.

About Renée Gendron

Renée Gendron writes romances. She has written fantasy romance, alternative history, and contemporary romances and has an eye on writing sci-fi and cyberpunk romances. When she isn't writing, she is taking courses or listening to books to hone her craft. She engages the writing community on Twitter through conversations on craft. She also extends structural edits.

Find out more about Renée Gendron below.

Website: reneegendron.com

Twitter: @ReneeGendron

Acknowledgments

Star Crossed came together as a brainchild of Renée Gendron with the support of D.W. Hitz. It was made possible by the hard work and amazing words of those authors who dedicated their time to create the preceding wondrous stories.

I'd like to thank each author and each member of their support systems for infusing their time, energy, and creativity into this project. As writers, we dedicate hours upon hours to our craft, and without the help and understanding of those around us, we would entirely run out of steam. Without the support of writers helping writers, many projects such as this would never get off the ground.

From Fedowar Press, I would like to say thanks once again to you, the reader, for spurring us onward. To B.K., Ian, Renée, Pamela, Nikki, J.L., and L.A., thank you for your enthralling words and endless imaginations.

Sincerely,
D.W. Hitz

What's Next?

Fedowar Press is hard at work on new stories in speculative fiction. Stay tuned for more content coming soon.

Stay up to date with our upcoming releases by checking out our website as well as our newsletter.

www.FedowarPress.com.